I0783581

# DOPEMAN

by

## MAURICE CAMPBELL

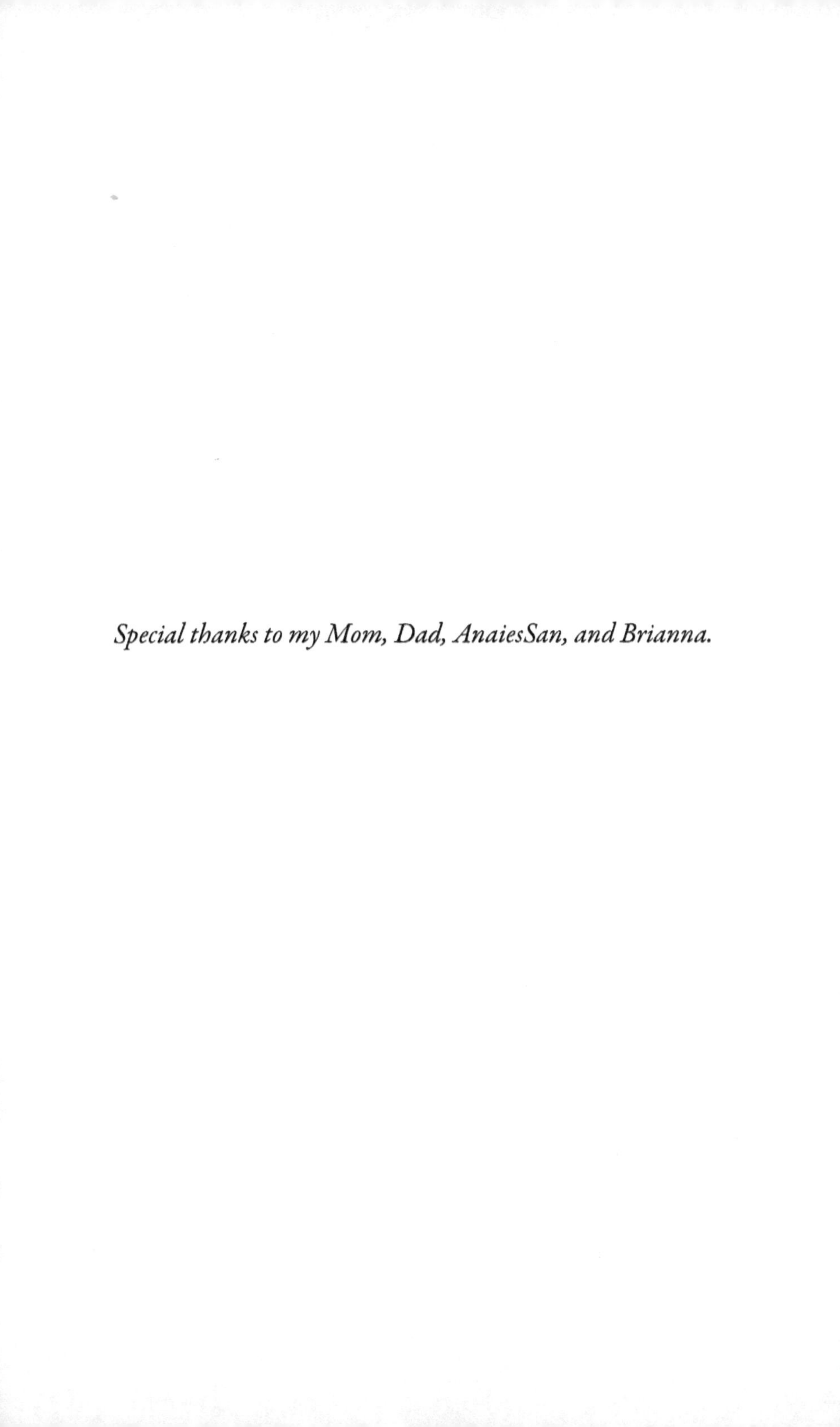

*Special thanks to my Mom, Dad, AnaiesSan, and Brianna.*

# INDEX

# PROLOGUE

## A WORLD ON FIRE

We kept pushing and innovating.

We made skyscrapers that could reach the heavens and trains that could go places in minutes instead of hours. We were always heading down this path. The technological revolution of 2002 accelerated our understanding of the internet and we surpassed countless milestones. By 2019, we had intelligent cities, hovercrafts, and the beginning of AI. The human race never looked better.

Until we looked worse.

The 2060s marked the beginning of the end. Resources were being used left and right to fuel those towns and tech. Some nations saw the writing on the wall. They would not be able to sustain these cities by decade's end.

We got desperate.

In 2079, German troops were stationed near Spain's source for oil. This was the spark. All it needed was...

The fuel.

On February 4th, 2080, Germany pushed against Spain, starting the Resource Wars in Europe. Unfortunately, the other countries saw an opportunity to seize all of the power for themselves, and made a desperate attempt to get as much as they could. It was World War III, but with no allies, no pride, and only the need for survival.

There was no good ending.

WWIII ended on June 22, 2082, with nukes. America nuked Germany, Japan nuked America, and the chain continued. There wasn't a nation that didn't feel Father Atom's touch. America was in shambles.

Ten years later, here we are. The west coast is a wild wasteland, a desert that's hot as hell. We haven't seen good rainfall in years.

But there is one man who stood tall and beat the odds to become the greatest.

His name?

Dopeman.

# CHAPTER ONE

## THE FOOLISH COURIER

The sun beamed down, and it felt like Satan himself was in bed with me.

Or something like that. I'm not a poet.

I opened my eyes yet again, starting another stressful day. It smelled of manure and sand. I'd gone to bed in a haystack, next to a horse. I had to get up quickly, however—I had a delivery to make and a reputation to uphold. I grabbed my dirty, faded shoes, my mail bag, and the package. It was tan, dusty, and unopened. Rule one in the courier's handbook: Never peek at the package. I waved goodbye to the horse, whom I'd dubbed Noah, and opened the barn door into (formerly) Compton, California.

It wasn't the same city after the Big Boom. It was a desert town now, like one of those wild west movies from the Old World. People used wagons and wore leather and cloth. Putting on my favorite bucket hat, I placed the package in my bag and strolled over to the water saloon. As soon as I opened the door the chatter slowed to a crawl.

The patrons looked at me.

 "What? Never seen a courier before? I'm looking for a Vermin Sellers. Is he here?" I asked the crowd.

One of the men spoke up. "Say... are you the Foolish Courier?"

"Yeah... Are you Vermin?" I responded, my eyebrows raised.

Everybody in the saloon looked tense. They slowly stood, and that was when I remembered that there was a bounty on me. How could I forget? The awkward silence had my anxiety going through the roof. This wasn't the first time I'd been in a shootout, but it always sucks to shoot at half of the damn town. Not wanting to kill anybody, I rolled out before they drew their guns. Knowing that the group was probably going to destroy the saloon, I ran across the street, loaded two high-volume explosive shells into my shotgun, and aimed. "This is your only warning! I just want to deliver a package!" I yelled as the group came out. They were about twenty deep.

"We're getting that 300,000 gold!" one of the patrons yelled back.

The cowboys were ready to shoot, that's a fact. Rifles, shotguns, even six-shooters, funny enough. I sighed as I hopped up over to my right, shooting the ground right in the middle of the group. The shell exploded on impact, with enough power to send some of the men flying, but they didn't die. I cocked back the shotgun to free the shell, and shot again, making the land blast out dirt and smoke. The joys of overloading a shotgun shell and adding a bit of military-grade explosive gel. Afterwards, I landed and pulled out my pistol, aiming as the smoke cleared. Four more men came out of the haze to attack me. Good news was they were too dazed to shoot me. I ran into the foursome, kicking and punching them in the head and gut to knock them out. *Geez... I can never get a break.*

"You've been busy, Courier," a voice behind me said. "I'm Vermin. You got my package?"

I nodded and handed him the package from my bag.

He smiled as he stared at it. "My dearest Ann. Thank you. Looks like the rumors are true about you, Foolish Courier."

"I hate that nickname..." I sighed. I'd had that dumb name for a while.

"To be fair, only a fool would be out in the open with a bounty that large," Vermin said, shaking my hand. "Oh, behind you!"

He turned to walk off. I looked around and aimed my shotgun with haste. There was a man with a pistol near one of the windows of the saloon. Shooting on instinct, I missed and hit the saloon on accident, causing it to explode, littering wood and glass over the dirt. *Damn explosive shells.*

The bartender peeked out of the new hole. "What the hell, man?!"

I had to get out of there before Miller Corps jumped on my ass.

# CHAPTER TWO
## MEET THE PRESS, DOPEMAN

What a day, I'll tell ya.

I never expected to blow up part of a saloon on the job, but here we are. I needed to get out of California, so I took the Desert Train. The train was constructed over five years by Miller Corps to supply their soldiers and make travel easier. The only problem was how expensive it was. Twenty gold per state? Geez. No wonder they controlled most of the west. However, it was that or walk to Nevada and be at the mercy of the heat, Desert Demons, and other punks wanting a shot at my bounty. Good thing I was only going there to get my payment, and there was a *no combat* rule on the train, so I was safe for now. After paying the fee, I got the paper ticket, and sat down in my seat next to the window. My eyelids became heavy. Being the paranoid man I was, I held my pistol at my hip as I closed my eyes, slipping into dreamland.

* * *

**"Hey, babe!"**

A female voice heightens my senses. I look around. There are... skyscrapers. Concrete. People in hoodies, jeans, and sneakers. Not dusters, tattered overalls, and cowboy boots. I smell the gas of vehicles and the aroma of popcorn from a nearby vendor. There's no doubt about it—I'm home. San Francisco. I look to my right, where somebody is clinging to my side. A woman. I can't see her face, everything was so blurry. All I can see is the color of her hair: white.

The girl with white hair kisses my cheek. It feels good. I feel relieved when I feel her warm lips bless my skin. I want her to kiss me again.

**"Let's go to the movies. I heard Love Note is on!"**

Her voice is at a perfect pitch. It's like a goddess speaking into my soul. I want her to talk forever. I blink, and she's gone. I look all around me, but suddenly all I see is sand. Now I'm home.

* * *

My eyes opened. I sighed and took a sip of my room-temperature water. It was gonna be a long trip.

I felt a tap on my shoulder. It was a woman, wearing a simple, white button-up shirt and soiled, brown slacks. She had suspenders, a brown press cap, and short, brown hair that matched her brown eyes. "Excuse me, are you the Foolish Courier?" she asked.

Judging by that hat, she wasn't a bounty hunter, so I leaned back in my seat. "Depends on who's asking."

The woman laughed. "I know it's you, Courier. I was just being nice."

I rolled my eyes. It wasn't hard to find me since I had a straw hat with a red stripe around it, and the name of my former girlfriend on the butt of my gun. "Sure. What do you want?"

"I'm Harper Atlas, of the Desertland News. I'm writing a story about the Foolish Courier and his exploits. Would you care to help me?"

"Depends," I responded, sipping my water. "What's in it for me?"

Harper pulled out a pair of slightly broken glasses and a notebook. "Well, your legend will be solidified! Who wouldn't want that?"

"Me. I'm not exactly a fan of Foolish Courier, anyways. I hate that nickname."

"How'd you get it in the first place? That'll be a good chapter!" Harper excitedly started to jot the title in her notebook.

With a sigh, I shook my head. I wasn't a fan of this story, but I told it anyway. "It was four years ago, on a delivery from New York to Miami. When I reached South Carolina, I caught a bounty. One thousand gold for property damage and resisting arrest. I was in a fight with someone. The prick was..." I clenched my fist. This was my least favorite part. "He was beating his daughter in the street, like badly. He started punching her. I had to stop him, so I kicked his ass. Turns out he was the sheriff. Got me locked up as soon as he could snap his fingers. I only had a week-long sentence, but I had to get this package delivered. I made a makeshift bomb to help me escape. I destroyed the cell wall, grabbed my gear, and left. Now they just keep coming after me in a vicious game of cat and mouse."

"Wow... You really are an idiot." Harper giggled as she finished writing in her notebook. "You only had a week! Was the job really that important?"

I scoffed and finished my water. "I'm not just any courier. I'm the guy who makes cross-country trips to get things done."

"Why even go through that much effort?"

"I have a reputation to uphold. It's all I have."

"No family, no friends?"

I responded with silence.

The train stopped at Badland, Nevada around midnight. Badland was a typical makeshift town with old broken houses, a small but useful hotel district, and a lot of working class citizens. The town itself wasn't bad; it was more of a warning to not go deeper into the state, since that was a lot more dangerous. I stepped off the train, with Atlas following. "You're not done?" I said, walking behind some locals in cowboy hats and dusty dresses.

"Of course not, Foolish Courier! We have so much to talk about!" Harper said excitedly, with stars in her eyes. I rolled my eyes as I reached the run-down house of my client.

Ann, my client, was happy to see me. She was a sad, stressed, middle-aged woman. Her brown hair was disheveled and she looked like she hadn't slept in days.

"Did he..." she started.

"Yes," I said, knowing what she was gonna say. "He loved it. And he loves you."

"T-Thank you!" Ann hugged me, crying.

After she paid me, I wandered toward the hotel district. It was time to reward myself.

Harper was still behind me. "So what was that about, Foolish Courier?"

"Can't say. Also, since you're gonna tell the world my story, I'm not the Foolish Courier."

"Ok." Harper nodded. "Then what's your name?"

I stopped and turned, giving a large grin and a superhero pose. "Call me Dopeman."

# CHAPTER THREE

## HARPER'S TALE

I had a good night's sleep and a good breakfast. Hadn't had those in months!

Of course my new journalist friend had rented a room next to mine and joined me at breakfast, asking me questions while I ate my demon eggs, which is the spiky green thing that Desert Demons lay. If you crack it open prematurely, it leaks the good stuff, like a chicken egg. I topped it off with a side of cactus juice.

"Why do you want to be called Dopeman?" she asked, scribbling in her notes.
Today she wore a red, button-up shirt, black slacks, matching black boots, and suspenders. With clean clothes, she was the definite standout of the hotel restaurant.

"I told you, you're not cool enough to know," I joked, taking big, sloppy bites of my food. It tasted more like sardines than something reptilian. *The power of genetic mutation.*

"What the hell? I'm cool! I mean, what's uncool about a journalist?"

"The fact that you have to ask that question answers your question."

"W-What? The hell does that even mean?"

"Exactly." I love to confuse folks. It's funnier than making actual jokes. Harper groaned and shook her head. I wiped my face clean and decided to play nice. "What's your story, then? You might have a rad backstory."

She looked surprised by my question. Had anybody ever asked about her life? "Well, before everything looked like this, I was in Texas. I lived on a ranch with my parents, but I loved to write and investigate. After a lot of resistance, I finally convinced them to let me go to college. I was a first-year student when the bombs fell. I never saw my parents after that…. I was the only person to make it to our bunker." She stopped for a moment to regain her composure. "I helped rebuild in my own way. I was out there, telling the world about the different creatures, the scandals, and NRF. There. I don't think it's cool, but it's my story."

I nodded. She certainly passed the cool test, though I didn't want to tell her yet. "Touching. You did a lot, didn't you?"

"Yeah, I did. So you have a story as well, considering your reputation."

Before I could retort, a woman walked up to us, avoiding eye contact. She clutched her dusty, tan skirt as she began to speak. "Excuse me… Are you the Foolish Courier? You can deliver anything? No matter what?"

I leaned back in my chair, pondering. "Well, depends on the price, miss. How much are ya willing to give me?"

"Eight hundred gold. All I need for you is to give this letter to Major Kyle Tann. He's in Southland."

Southland, Nevada, the former Las Vegas, was a dangerous place for people like me. Tons of bloodthirsty bandits and creatures waiting to claim my head, for money or food. Maybe even both. "Major Kyle. What army is he fighting for? Why would he be in Southland of all places? Pretty sure that's labeled Godless on the map." Godless towns. A Miller Corps phrase for lawless, conflicted towns. The bad boy places that had yet to embrace rules and order.

"He's Miller Corps. He won't tell me what he's doing there, some kind of classified operation." The woman shifted her gaze to the ground. "Can you do it, sir?"

Miller Corps. Everyone's favorite independent army. They fought to make America like it was before the bombs dropped. "Yeah. Give me the letter." The woman sighed with relief, smiling. Seemed like she'd been asking other people for a while now. She gave me the letter, and I got up. Harper was writing silently.

"How are you gonna make it in Southland with a bounty that large?" Harper inquired, following me out of the restaurant.

"Oh, that's easy! I'll ask the army for help, of course!" Why wouldn't Miller Corps help their own soldiers?

The walk was a little long, giving me a chance to get a good look at the town during the day. Having been here a lot, I knew Badlands was just a passover town. The working class men and women shuffled to work, from building houses to shopkeeping and playing peacemaker as the Miller Corps policed the area. It was a friendly town. As one of the closest to Southland, Badlands' new purpose was to be used as a supply town, with many of the soldiers scrambling to get supplies for the caravans headed down to give military support. This made the makeshift barracks easy to slip into.

I hopped over to the barracks, which seemed to be the army headquarters for this town. Walking into one of the big tents, I approached the assistant behind the front desk.

"I'm Dopeman, and I have to send an urgent letter to Major Kyle Tann."

The assistant raised his eyebrow and called somebody over.

"Dopeman, is it?" A soldier came out from behind a partition. "I'm Commander Green. What's in this letter that is so important?" Green was tall and middle-aged. His stubble was graying and a bad scar ran across his left cheek, from his lower lip to the bottom of his eyelid. Almost messed up his emerald eye. He had this natural, bored look about him. He kept a constant frown with low eyelids.

"It's for him. Not me." I showed the letter off, letting him see the envelope labeled Tann.

"Hm. Why tell us, then? Give it to him."

"See, that's the issue. I'm... Foolish Courier."

"Ah..." Green nodded and scratched his chin. "The courier with the bounty on his head. Heard you blew up a saloon from one of our men fresh off the train. Dangerous man, I must say. You know how much property you destroyed?" Harper looked at me; she could tell I was losing him.

"That wasn't my fault, sir. See, some dudes wanted my head, so I defended myself."

Green looked at me with disappointment. "By blowing up a saloon?"

"Yes. But that's not the point! You want Kyle to complete his mission or not?" A bit of a lie, but I had to get my foot in the door.

The commander scoffed and shook his head. "We can't supply you with any men, if that's what you're asking. We're much too busy here. But If you have to go to Southland, there is a caravan scheduled to leave later today. If you offer to guard it, there's your protection. We get one free man over here, and you'd head into town. Sounds good?"

Harper tapped my shoulder. "I can't go that deep into Godless territory, so I'll wait here. Make sure you tell me everything!"

I shook Green's hand and he took me to the caravan—and most likely my death.

# CHAPTER FOUR
## THE ROAD WITH NO SOUL. PART ONE

*"Yo! **Dopeman!** You got that stuff, my G?"*

*"**Dopeman!** Sling the rock my way, youngblood!"*

*"**Dopeman!** Baby! I d-don't got the money right now, b-but I need that magic baby..."*

*They didn't know my **name**. Nobody did. After a while, I **forgot** it myself. Nobody would remind me. I was just an object to them. I always got the job done. That's what everybody used me for, anyway. I'd shill dope, make people laugh. Whatever I did to make **people feel better.** It hurts when you **stop laughing at your own jokes.** I couldn't remember, but she helped me. The girl with the **white** hair. She always said my name.*

*What is my **name?***

*Who am I?*

Opening my eyes, I remembered where I was—on the road to Southland. The caravan was bringing vital medical supplies Miller Corps needed for the war. There was only one official path on the map, with "Soulless Road" as a cute nickname scribbled over the line of the Old World path. The road wasn't paved; it had been carved out by humans and creatures alike on the road to the most famous Godless town. I had to keep my eyes peeled for raiders and Desert Demons. Since the driver and I had agreed it was relatively safe, I was sitting in the back resting with two other folks: a rather buff young woman with a massive revolver, and an elder. I was moving my feet, bored out my mind, making a beat with the tapping of my shotgun.

After a bit, the old coot tapped my shoulder. "That's a pretty nice piece right there," he mumbled. His voice was deep. Commanding, but still old.

"Oh? Thanks! It's an old war shotty that I modified myself. It can take custom shells. It's pretty easy to make shells and gunpowder," I replied. Through years of practice I was becoming a master at tinkering.

The elder looked shocked. "Custom shells? What kinda shells?"

"Explosive, demon killer, nonlethal, armor-piercing... The usual. I got other stuff too. Flashbangs, smoke bombs, ya know?" Well, there was a little more than that. I just didn't want to bore him.

The young woman spoke up with a strong southern accent. "With a shotgun that impressive, I'm surprised you're not a gunsmith."

I chuckled and shook my head. "Wasn't in the cards for me. I just like tweaking things. Making stuff better." I looked over at her large six-shooter. "Speaking of surprises, I'm surprised you're not a proper bodyguard with muscles like that."

She laughed. "I owe the old man my life. He wanted to resupply the boys in Southland, so here I am."

"I told you"—The old feller coughed—"Ah. I told you I didn't want you risking your life. We got plenty of protection. What's your name again?"

"I told you. Dopeman."

"No, like your real name, son."

As I thought about it, the wagon suddenly shook. I heard howling and shrieking outside.

"D-Demons!" the driver yelled.

We jumped out to see the full scope of everything. The horses were too spooked to continue. Surrounded by sand and dead trees, I loaded my demon killer shells, heard a whooshing noise over my head, and barely dodged a spear. Damn, it was Desert Demons.

Desert Demons were humanoid-looking horntoads who evolved incorrectly. They gained enough intelligence to create their own language, and they hated humans.

I saw one of the gray bastards and shot. I missed, and the creature yelled out, causing the other six to come down from the decaying trees. They all held bone knives, ready to kill. I was ready to kill too, so we had one thing in common.

"Erap! Forgrth!" a demon barked out.

On command, two charged at me from either side. I smacked the one on my left with the butt of my gun while spinning out the way of the blow from the one on my right. I spun behind him, shotgun aimed at his head.

"Special delivery!" I yelled as I sent the demon to the hellscape he came from.

The other one attempted to get up, but I kicked it in the face and sent it to the underworld as well. Once that was over, I looked up to help the others.

The buff woman was putting her left arm to work. Panting heavily, she killed two more with her massive gun. She was going for a third, but one of the demons knocked the gun out of her hand. Since I was close enough to show off, I struck the demon with a flying dropkick, then shot two slugs to the monster's chest to save her. I looked up, smiled, then continued my mission. The driver was being assaulted by multiple demons who used their spears and claws to cut and beat on the man. I ran up to shoot one in the back, and filled the other with lead from my pistol. After four shots to the back and one to the chest, it finally went down. I was whacked, looking around for... Wait, there was one more.

There was the last demon, leaping towards the muscled woman. My eyes went wide. I had no time to reload, no time to warn her, and she was too tired to move. She was going to die. Suddenly, the old man was in the way of the blade. It impaled his chest. I shoved a shell in and shot the demon dead.

"DORIAN!" she wailed, hugging the old man hard.

We grouped around her and saw her breaking down, a natural response to someone you know dying in brutal fashion in front of you. She shook and let her emotions go. Endless tears and blood stained her face as the rest of us could do nothing, watching her mourn in her own way.

Least somebody knew his name before he died.

# CHAPTER FIVE
## THE ROAD WITH NO SOUL, PART TWO

*O God, I ask for **forgiveness.***

*I ask for my **salvation** like you have saved many others before.*

*You see me, you see my **pain.***

*Why must you see me in **pain?***

*Is it because I **ruined my community** with the **drugs** I sold?*

***Save me,** dear lord.*

*I'm **running out of time.***

*Amen.*

My eyes opened as I unclenched my hands. Taking a deep sigh, I looked back to see the small caravan camp I made with the remaining group. Got their names too, which was nice. There was Fisher, the injured driver, and Sera, the gunslinger. Sera was broken by Dorian's death—she couldn't even give him a proper burial.

After we packed up the camp, we moved on to the second leg of the trip. I was in the passenger seat with Fisher, guarding the wagon, until he suggested that I take a quick break to check on Sera. She was staring at the floor, seemingly trying to distract herself. Once I sat down, I scooted closer, taking off my bucket hat to reveal my curly hair. "Talk to me," I started.

She snapped out of her trance, looking up at me. "W-What? What do you want?"

"He must've meant a lot to you. I've heard talking about these kinds of things helps us cope easier. Or something like that," I laughed nervously. It had been a while since I talked to anybody about loss.

She noticed my awkwardness. She flipped her short, blonde hair. "He was the only thing I had left. Dorian took care of me after we resurfaced. I was scared, I'll be honest. My family didn't make it, my friends were gone. I had absolutely nothing." Tears welled up in her eyes, and I put an arm around her. "I was living not knowing if I'd see tomorrow. It was so much pain. Then I met Dorian. He was an old man with a heart of gold, I swear. He took me in, taught me how to properly shoot. In return, I'd work out and make sure he was protected. I loved him. Now he's..."

"I understand, Sera. It's gonna be hard moving on, but you can do it. I know you can."

She turned to me, eyes welling with tears. "How? I have nobody left."

"You can always find new people. There's so many in this new world, looking for a friend." I smiled. "Chin up. I know he doesn't like you sad."

Sera sighed, wiping her face. "Thanks, Dopeman. While I doubt it... I'll think about it."

"And that's the first step to change."

An hour later, we reached the home stretch. The outskirts of Southland had seen better days. The area was covered in ruined buildings, cracked roads, and smoke from old fires. It looked like a battle had taken place recently, due to all the corpses littering the area. Fisher slowed the horse in case anything came out at us. For a while, everything was cool. Then a raider walked into the middle of the street.

Fisher stopped the wagon.

"People! I heard you're moving crates around. We need those supplies," the raider called.

"I'm sorry, we're not giving these to you!" Fisher yelled back.

Meanwhile, I was crouching in the back with Sera. "These guys are trouble. I need to get rid of them," I said with confidence.

Sera scoffed. "It'll be more trouble if you go. Now just stay back and—"

"Nonsense! I got this. When I say get down, you get down, okay?" I hopped out, ignoring Sera's protestations.

I walked around the side of the caravan. "Didn't you hear what he said? They're not for you to take." I loaded my shotgun, looking mean.

Once he saw my hat, he realized who he was looking at. "Wait... You're Foolish Courier! It's payday, boys! GET EM!" the raider roared. His gang popped out of the surrounding buildings from above. *Whoops.*

I reached for my belt to get a flashbang. Hastily pulling the pin and tossing it into the air, I shouted a quick warning to the others and averted my gaze.

Fisher and Sera threw themselves flat as a giant ball of light lit up the gang. The raiders couldn't see much, but they saw enough to shoot at the caravan.

"Go! I'll find my own way!" I yelled, rolling in the opposite direction.

Once Fisher got back in the driver's seat, he whipped the horse into a gallop and I spotted Sara leering out from the window as they streamed past. She looked upset, but I'd live with it. Maybe.

I then loaded a high explosive slug and shot at one of the dilapidated buildings to make it half-collapse. The ground shook violently, and a combination of rubble and glass made a dust cloud on impact. Taking advantage of the chaos and confusion, I sprinted to the other side of the building and hopped on one of the raider's horses. Heels dug in deep, I rode into the wind.

Unfortunately, my plan wasn't spotless. After a few minutes, I heard the clopping and the labored breathing of a horse on my tail. I turned to see an angry raider, ready and willing to take my head. I urged my horse to go faster but it resisted, bucking its head and snorting angrily.

The raider caught up and tackled me into the sandy shoulder of the road. We tumbled down the slope and my shotgun slid away. He mounted me and started beating my face in. I was too dazed to react, but after the third punch bloodied my nose, I threw sand in his face and kicked him off. Stumbling to my feet with another fistful, I charged at him, but he dodged. *He's smarter than I thought.*

He kneed me twice to the stomach, but I retorted with an elbow to his face, breaking his nose. My ribs started to hurt; my nose was burning with pain. I had to end this. I faked a blow to the head to go straight for the money makers, hitting him in the groin. It was pretty easy after that—two swift knees to the head and a boot to the face. He collapsed on the ground, out cold. I didn't want to kill anybody else, so I left him there. I sighed as I checked my nose. Not broken, but it hurt like hell.

Grabbing my gun, I went up the slope only to see the horse still standing there, surprisingly. It appeared to be pretty tired and hungry. I could see her ribs through her once golden coat, which was now ruined by scars and mistreatment.

I approached it slowly, hand out. "Hey"—I did a quick peek under her belly—"girl, I just need a ride. I know you're starving. You help me out and I get you food. Deal?"

She looked down for a moment, then back at me, nodding.

"Ok, let's go. I'll think of a name later. I'm just a bit messed up at the moment," I said with a weak smile. The adrenaline was wearing off.

Staggering over and mounting her, we rode to the gates of Southland.

Beyond the gates were the former outskirts of the Las Vegas strip, now reduced to a handful of dusty tents where Miller Corps housed their sick.

Once I made my way to a tent, Sera ran up to me furiously. "Why in the hell would you do that?! You could've been killed!"

"You're weren't, were you?" I responded, holding my nose.

"I'm not talking about me or Fisher. I'm talking about you. Why make these dumb choices? Is that how you got that nickname? You're one dumb choice from death!"

"Is that supposed to be a bad thing?"

# CHAPTER SIX
## ONE NIGHT IN SOUTHLAND

I was holed up for the next few hours in a medical area as doctors tended to my fractured nose and bruised ribs. They said I'd be fine if I rested for a day or two. I attempted to do just that, lying in bed and reading a book about how to change my guns and gadgets. I'd been there for a couple of hours when Sera walked in to check on me.

She sat on the bed, head hanging low. "Dopeman..." she said quietly.

"Yeah? You alright, Sera?" I asked, sitting up and holding my damaged ribs.

"I should be asking that question. You could've died today. Why do something that dangerous?"

I rolled my eyes. "You already asked this. I wanted you two out."

"What about you? How would you have gotten out? Dumb luck?"

"I call it classic gambler's luck, but to each their own." I laughed.

She wasn't amused. "You're hurt, Dopeman. I can see—"

I raised my hand to stop her. "No... No. I didn't pay for a therapy session. Sorry."

Sera stood. "Fine, that's fair. Could you pay for a drink tonight? Me and Fisher are going."

I pondered, scratching my stubble. I had no plans. Folks around had told me that Tann wasn't going to be in Southland till the next day. As long as I didn't do anyting too dumb, I figured I'd be fine to go drinking at least. I shrugged. "Sure. Just no funny stuff, yeah?"

She nodded and left me to my own devices.

Later that night, I walked around the Southland strip. Surprisingly, Vegas had been restored to its former glory. It was filled with brothels, casinos, and bars with actual booze; alcohol was a rare thing to see since not a lot of people wanted to be dehydrated. I saw Sera and Fisher, both dressed like settlers in their ragged clothes. Sera hugged me and Fisher shook my hand, finally giving me a good look at the middle-aged driver. He had a long, brown beard, and dirty straight hair.

We went into a club to drink. It was my first time drinking an alcoholic drink, so yay new experiences. I knocked back a shot and gagged. It tasted like rubbing alcohol, and it burned in my throat. Fisher chuckled as he finished his own drink.

Two shots in and I was already feeling something. The music, the people chattering... Starting to feel a little drowned out, I put my chin in my hand and called to Fisher. "Hey, I don't think I asked, but what made you come to Godless territory?"

He shrugged. "Well, I like money. Plus looking at Sera is always a benefit." He gawked at her.

Sera rolled her eyes and turned to me. "*This* guy... I can never get rid of him."

Fishier winked at her. "What can I say, I like my women buff."

Four shots and we were all tipsy. Fisher fell asleep on the stool, so Sera led me to a quiet area in the back to talk. The booths were small, made for couples. We sat shoulder to shoulder against the wall.

"So," Sera started, "you're Foolish Courier?"

"Yeah. Why?"

"It seems you have a history of doing dumb things. Blowing up saloons, shooting up entire enemy bases, falling off high places for packages..."

"I get it," I groaned. "Is this going somewhere?"

"You keep risking your life for other people. Why?"

I reluctantly answered the question. "God... I just think I owe somebody something. I didn't exactly help anybody out in the Old World. I did the opposite. If I die for somebody else to live, I can finally forgive myself."

Sera hugged me. She felt warm. "You need to forgive yourself. You think you have nothing to lose, but... what if you lose me?" she asked. She looked me straight in the eyes.

I chuckled and got up. My face felt hot. I hoped she didn't see me blush. "Come on, let's wake Fisher up."

Going back to the bar, we saw that he was already up, drunkenly arguing with some tall skinhead about the seat he was sleeping in.

I stepped up. "What's the issue? Let's just drink, fellas."

"This doesn't concern you, boy." The skinhead pushed me.

*Ok, he's on strike two already.*

"The hell was that for?" Fisher pushed the skinhead back, who then punched Fisher in retaliation.

*Strike three.*

I grabbed the bottle, hopped on the dude's back, and smashed it over his head. The large man tried his best to buck me off by crashing through tables and into walls, but I held on to his neck, doing anything I could to take him out, but nothing worked.

"Knock him out!" Sera yelled.

"CAN'T YOU SEE I'M TRYING?!"

Apparently I wasn't trying hard enough. The skinhead was yelling in frustration; he had to finish this before he passed out. Like a madman, he charged though the window with no mind for safety. We crashed through it and landed in the water troughs. A crowd formed in a circle, laughing at me and the senseless man. Looking up at the sky, I thought to myself:

*I'm never drinking again.*

# CHAPTER SEVEN
## WAR SUCKS! [AND HERE'S WHY]

Last night hadn't done my ribs too many favors. In fact, it did the exact opposite.

I hated this town.

I didn't remember much of anything after the window stunt, but Serena, my new horse, headbutted me awake. I jerked up, holding my pounding head. I was in a barn, apparently. It was pretty small, and had a wide open clearing for the animals. Only this time, it was empty aside from Serena.

Looking down, I saw I had a note on my chest.

"Your horse dragged you here. She seemed pretty protective of you, so we left you with some painkillers and left. Give us a call when you're up!

—Sera"

"You could've taken me to the medical tent, ya know," I said to Serena.

She neighed at me angrily.

"I know, I know. Thank you. I'll give you two apples today."

A pleading whinny escaped her mouth.

"Fine, three. Can't say no to you." I petted her. She seemed happy.

"I gotta go to work now, okay?" I whispered.

I snagged three apples from a nearby table and gave them to Serena. I left, popping a painkiller to ease the pain in my ribs.

From the books I'd read about horses, Serena was an Akhal-Teke. She was a rare sight in the west, must've been here pre-war. Her dark, golden shine was a great appeal to most. We'd only met a day or two ago, but I liked her. She seemed to feel the same. Must've been hell back at those raider camps. Ever since I gave her a name and food, she seemed to trust me.

It was another hot day in Nevada; triple digits at least. If It wasn't for my water canister and hat, I would've been baked. *When is it going to rain?*

I walked over to the Miller Corps area of town. It was filthy, like the people purposely littered here. Graffiti was all over the destroyed walls, telling the army to go back home to Cali. The rest weren't as nice, with slurs and other rude comments. The guards were also high-strung, aiming their guns at me as soon as I was in sight. I flashed the courier's bag and they started yelling.

"Who's the mail for, courier?"

"Major Kyle Tann. From his lover," I said.

One of them walked into the tent behind them. After a few moments, he returned, giving the all-clear signal. I then walked into said tent and saw Major Kyle Tann for the first time.

Tann was younger than most, maybe in his mid-to-late 20s. He was leaning on a table, back to me, looking at a map of the local area. "Dopeman, aka Foolish Courier. Fisher told me what you did with those Desert Demons and raiders. Nice work out there."

Tann turned around to shake my hand. He was clean-shaven, but he had heavy bags under his eyes. His black hair was short and shaggy, and mostly covered by his green beret. "Now, I assume my wife sent me something?"

I nodded and handed him the letter.

He read it over and looked shocked. "It seems that... I'm a father. I got more waiting for me back home." He put the paper down and sat down for a drink of water, quickly soaking in the information.

"Congrats, man. I hope you'll see them soon."

I gave a quick bow and turned to leave, but Tann stopped me. "Ah, Dopeman. Before you leave, I understand there's a bounty on you, right?"

I turned and raised my eyebrow. "Yeah, why?"

"Must be hard to do a job with a 400,000 gold bounty on your head."

"I've been managing so far."

"Only a matter of time before that luck runs out."

I folded my arms. "What are you getting at, Major?"

He was short and sweet. "I want you to help us claim this land. We need Southland for tactical advantage against the NRF."

"Ah yes, the Nation of Righteous Fighting. Listen, I don't have a horse in this race. I'm not a fan of war."

"You won't be in the war itself, don't worry. I just need help with an operation. Godless are running wild on the west coast. I see nothing of the sort in the east. The NUSA government needs to come over here…" He paused.

The New United States of America government had yet to come to the wild west. We only knew of its existence because of travelers from the east looking for freedom, or an excuse to do whatever they wanted. Miller Corps was only a force looking to restore democracy against the NRF, which was looking for the opposite.

"We're getting tired of constant animalistic behavior here!" Kyle looked passionate. "This war against the raiders is necessary. The war on the NRF is a requirement."

"War this, war that. All war will ever do is lead people to more and more death. You can't control these people, man. Society as we know it is dead now. I'll help fight. Just clear my damn bounty."

I felt uncomfortable agreeing to take part in a war. I also wasn't a fan of having the bounty used against me. Afterall, they were the ones who calculated the damages and added them on to my total number.

"Great. Come back in about a week. We'll move out then."

I left and walked over to the regular part of town, to a much smaller bar to chill with Sera and Fisher for a few hours. I told them what happened.

"This is great!" Sera yelled while drinking her water. She almost choked.

Fisher agreed. "With our help, we can crush anything. Cheer up."

"Wait." I snapped out of my slump and looked up. "Our?"

"Yeah, we're joining you. There's no way I'm letting you die out there," Sera said.

Fisher chuckled. "If only you could say that to me."

Sera turned to him. "Shut up before I choke you."

"Please do…" he replied, practically drooling at the threat.

"Alright!" I shouted. I did not want to go down that path. "If you want to join, fine. God, I hate war."

Sera leaned in. "Who doesn't? War can go die in a fire."

"If it wasn't for war, I would be in my house, with her. She's skull and bones now. Because of war. Because of these damned bombs," I ranted.

"Who's she?"

"Dani. My girlfriend."

I stood and left. I didn't feel like talking about Dani—the girl with the white hair.

# CHAPTER EIGHT
## THE GIRL WITH THE WHITE HAIR

**Dani.**

**Dani Hikari.**

How could I forget that name? She saved my life.

I grew up living in San Francisco with my mother. I was fifteen when she had a miscarriage. I tried my best to help her, I truly did. I'd cook, clean, and sacrifice my grades in school to take her places after that. Despite all of that, she resented me for being unemployed and treated me like I was worthless. She'd still yell at me and beat me over the smallest things. At sixteen, I moved out.

For the month that I was homeless, I made friends with a few homeless people and others down on their luck. I started helping our little community by getting food and protecting it from gangs. I was surviving, not living, however. I needed work. I just wanted to know where my next meal was coming from. Some sketchy dude wanted me to sell some weed as a favor. With no options left, I said yes, and for the first time in my life, I made my own money. It was $130. It felt so good. Soon I was a mainstay, selling to a few kids and oldheads to get me a lower-end apartment on the shady side of town.

When more competition stepped into the game, I made less money, putting my cushy lifestyle in jeopardy. Needing to step things up a notch, I contacted an old plug named Donte.

"Yo, what's the word?" Donte said as he stepped into my den.

I looked out the window, determined. "Yeah. Imma sell crack now. I need people."

"Woah, crack? You know what happens if we get pinched with crack, dawg?"

"Same thing with weed—jail. You know the risks regardless, bro. I ain't snitchin' and I put that on everything I love. I just need help pushing it."

Donte sighed. "Fine. But don't say I ain't warn you."

A few months later, I was balling. High-end apartments, gold chains, and the women. I had it all. All I had to do was ruin the community with what I sold. I would walk around the old parks I used to play in. All I saw were baseheads and bums smoking up. Dopeman got rich off these fool's backs, simple as that.

That sent me into a deep depression. I was smoking a cigarette one night, leaning against the rails on the Golden Gate Bridge. I was thinking about jumping, actually. There was gonna be another Dopeman. Another man to take my place when I'm gone.

**"Hey."** I heard a woman behind me.

**"What's your name?"** she asked. I turned to face her. She had white hair. **"I'm Dani Hikari."**

I was slightly surprised at the question. "D-Dopeman. The streets call me the Dopeman."

**"I'm not asking what the streets call you. What's your actual name?"**

I told her my name. I can't remember it.

**"Oh! I like that name. I'm calling you that from now on, okay?"**

I nodded and started smiling. Why was my heart beating so fast?

Oh, yeah.

The girl with the white hair had stolen my heart.

# CHAPTER NINE
## CLEAN HOUSE

Over the week I made a home in the barn to keep Serena company. I wanted to lie low from any lawless freak that thought they were lucky. I just had to ignore the goats blaring at night, and I'd made a deal with the farmer to have the goats out during the day. When a letter arrived from Harper, I settled with my lady horse and started reading.

"Hey! I was wondering if you're even still alive down there. I've heard rumors that a certain Dopeman blew up half a building to get rid of some raiders. I really wish you wouldn't do dumb stuff like that. You got people who need you. Like me! How else can I tell the legend of Dopeman if Dopeman dies? So, write me back when you can. If not, you better say something when you get back!

—Harper"

Serena nudged me, huffing.

I stood to pet her. "You're right, I should write her back."

I put the paper on an old, hay-littered table that held farming tools and started writing.

"Yo! I'm alive, don't worry. I'm happy you even thought to write. I appreciate it a lot. You know me, I always want to see people safe, but I'll try to stay safe myself. When I get back to town, I promise to tell you everything. Enough about me—I hope you're thriving, doing the good work you've been doing already. Keep safe!

Your favorite fool,

Dopeman."

After taking the letter to the post office, I rode to the Miller Corps camp to get my information from Tann. Fisher was having a smoke while the other soldiers got ready. "Morning, Fisher," I said, dismounting and proceeding to lean next to him.

He turned to me and grinned. "Hey, Dopeman. Today's the day, eh?"

"Guess it is. You know what to do?"

"Not a clue." Fisher flicked the cig away, shrugging. "I was told to follow your lead."

"Speaking of, where's Sera?"

Fisher pointed to one of the many wagons. "She's getting her ammo stocked up."

I nodded and headed into the tent. Kyle was drinking water and polishing his assault rifle. With weaponry like that, it was clear that Miller Corps had tons of pre-war weaponry saved up, which would explain how much of California they took.

"Dopeman, welcome," he said coldly.

I sat in a nearby chair and scoffed. "What? No hug and kiss?" I chuckled, but Kyle kept a straight face. "You got the information for me?"

He set the map and other notes down. "Operation Usurp Heaven will be taking place over many days. Starting today, we'll camp right here in the unmarked village. We'll be calling it Mother Base for the time being. It'll be in striking distance of our foe, Tribe Trastorno."

The Major opened another folder containing a few pictures of men stationed around a two-story house. Its caved-in roof had been patched with sturdy pieces of wood and the broken windows were taped up. Basically, a trap house. I assumed those raiders did the repairs. "These tribe members plan to disrupt our attempt to bring order and some form of normalcy to the west coast. Your mission is to take your team and free this house. There are rumors of slaves and drug mules here. They benefit from this place, so it needs to go."

After looking at the information, I nodded and left. Strangely, he didn't tell me to free anyone. *I'll just do the freeing myself then.*

* * *

A few hours later, the moon hung high in the sky and we were camped over at Mother Base. It seemed to be some sort of deserted village with poorly built buildings made of sand and mud. Sera, Fisher, and I stepped off the wagon, wasting no time getting to work as the rest of the army went to do their own missions.

"We need a team name," Fisher said as we mounted our horses to ride over to the Trastorno slave house.

I agreed. "Team Dopeman, easy."

Sera scoffed. "Of course you want the team to be named after you. I say we should be Team Gunslinger!"

Fisher shook his head. "Nah, I think we should be Team Badass! Like, I think that's a good way to show how good we are!"

"If you're five, yeah," Sera mumbled.

"Oh, I'll show you what's five—"

"Enough, children!" I interrupted.

We rode the rest of the way in silence. The cool night air was a welcomed treat after spending hours in the baking sun.

I stopped when we crested the top of a hill. Taking out a broken pair of binoculars with cracked lenses, I surveyed the house . "Eight dudes. Two in the front, the rest are inside. Nothing I can't handle."

Fisher readied his sniper rifle. "Do we have a plan?"

I made a face and chuckled. "Plans are for suckers. Just go with the flow. I'll slide down, you two just back me up."

Sera shook her head. "Wait, no—"

"Great! Good luck, team!" I slid down the hill, loading my new Devil's Kiss fire shells into my shotgun.

From the bottom of the hill, I ran up and popped the two guards in the head with my pistol. I kicked the door in as my team shot at the second door. There were two in the kitchen, and I made sure they were cooked well done—courtesy of the new slugs. As I marveled at my handiwork, someone grabbed my shoulders from behind and rammed my head through an unbroken window. I kicked the dude in the stomach for space and took aim, but he was quick to react. Grabbing my shotgun by the barrel, he wrenched it from my clutches, and tossed it aside. I attempted to swing at him, but he caught my waist and slammed me to the hardwood floor. He mounted me and wrapped his hands around my neck. I felt air escape my lungs; I struggled to find anything I could use to get his big ass off me.

Thankfully, a gunshot went off and the tribesman slumped against me. I kicked him off and finished him with my own pistol, struggling to catch my breath.

Sera helped me up and we searched the house. Upstairs, three dead men were heaped in a pile—her and fisher's handy work. Downstairs, Fisher got the house ready for burning, but he noticed there was a small hatch under.

"There's something here!"

It led down to a basement crammed with people—traumatized slaves and junkies in little better than a dark hole. We escorted them out of the house and Fisher set it on fire.

Sera patched my bloody face as I studied the giant fire. "Thank you," I said.

Sera shook her head and smiled. "Team Foolish," she replied.

I coughed and looked at her in confusion. "Why call ourselves Team Foolish?"

"Because we're foolish enough to follow you, Dopeman."

# CHAPTER TEN

## HOLY WAR

We rode back to Mother Base as soon as the house smoldered behind us. Eventually, the rest of the Miller Corps companies came back from their missions. They all had success, so we celebrated. Everyone drank booze to celebrate the first day of Usurp Heaven going off without a hitch—I stuck to water.

Leaning on a barrel, I watched the soldiers party. They knew how to get down, and I loved the fast-paced music. They probably danced and moved like this because it'd be the last time for a while, or even at all for some of them. I saw Fisher moving with another buff woman—the smile plastered on his face was huge. Weirdly, I couldn't see Sera anymore, and Kyle sat next to me. "While I'm not a fan of my soldiers getting drunk, it's a good morale boost," he said.

"What's wrong with drinking? They're enjoying themselves."

"Humans are creatures of habit; once you get something you enjoy in your system, you'll use it over and over."

"You don't trust your own people?"

Kyle scoffed. "I don't trust anyone, Dopeman." He stood and patted my back. "Good job out there today. I'll have something planned for tomorrow." He walked away, leaving me to sip my water alone.

Sera came up to me, her hand outstretched. The light gave a sparkle to her eyes and an angelic shine to her hair. "Hey, Dopeman. Let's dance."

I laughed. "Just a warning, I suck."

The song changed to a low-fi tune. I took her hand and held her tight as we slowly danced. Resting my cheek on her head, I felt Sera's heartbeat slow. Her beautiful, blonde hair smelled familiar, like something I'd been missing. It was alluring. We swayed from side to side as the lights shone, feeling like we were alone.

"What was she like?" Sera whispered.

"Who?" I whispered back.

"Dani. What was she like?"

Dani was my savior. She helped me realize something I couldn't see without her help. She would pick me up when I was down, and remind me that I'm more than a tool."

"What did you do in the past?"

I sighed. "I sold drugs, ruined my community. It's hard to forgive yourself when you've done that. Especially when you're only known as the man who supplied them."

Sera stopped and looked me straight in the eyes. "You need to. You can't keep trying to hurt yourself to protect us because you feel guilty for what happened all those years ago. You're a new man."

I started to tear up. "I can't. I killed all those people and profited from them. I was only known as that. As the Dopeman. She reminded me who I was. I can't remember now. Who am I, Sera? Who the hell am I?"

She placed her warm hands on my cheeks and wiped my tears away with her thumbs. "How about I remember for you?"

We softly placed our foreheads together as I cried. My emotions rushed out like water escaping a broken pipe. She comforted me for the rest of the party. When she invited me to her tent, I denied the offer. It didn't feel right.

* * *

Tann woke me up the next morning. Serena looked like she was gonna hurt the Major, so I made a hand signal to calm her down. "Morning, Dopeman. Today, you and I are going to do our own mission."

I sat up and pulled my boots on. "What? Why us? Why not my team?"

Kyle shrugged. "I want to see how you work in person."

"What aren't you telling me, Major?"

"Nothing. We leave in five." Like a true soldier, he turned on his heel and walked away. *God, this is going to be a pain.*

Five minutes later, we were riding off to the target. Kyle cleared his throat. "Trastornos got a drug den over to the west of Mother Base. It's also a common meeting place. Just like yesterday, clean house."

I kept silent. While I did hate dealers, I felt bad when it came to addicts. Especially those in the wastelands. No hope for life to return to normal, just to have it ripped away by drugs.

We took our horses to the rocky hills of Nevada. Tann and I reached a cliff overlooking the place. I studied the Trastornos. They wore leather armor and their faces were tattooed based on rank. The more tattoos they had, the more respected they were. A heavily tattooed one entered, and they all bowed. Kyle tapped my shoulder. "We'll rappel down. They won't expect an attack in the middle of the day."

We set up our ropes and rappeled down the cliff face. Once we touched the ground we snuck over to the side of the den. It looked to be the remains of a church with a collapsed roof. Peeking inside a window, I saw soldiers and followers alike on their knees, praying. There were ten people in total. It hit me: This was a place of worship, not a drug den.

I turned to warn Kyle. He already had a bomb lit.

"Move!" he yelled as he threw it.

I dove out of the way as it went off. The explosion rocked what was left of the building, destroying one side of the wall and causing the building to collapse. Kyle took his assault rifle and double tapped the bodies of soldiers and civilians alike as he stepped into the rubble of the church.

"This is what you hid from me? This was a place where they worshiped their gods!" I yelled, walking in the destroyed building.

"I knew you wouldn't do it. The rest of the companies had important stuff to do, so this fell to you naturally. I had a plan B if you couldn't barge in there like you usually would."

"Why me?!" I shouted, pointing at my chest.

"To show you this isn't a damn game! Real lives are at stake, Dopeman!"

I kicked a piece of the destroyed wall out of frustration.

War. What was it good for?

Absolutely nothing.

# CHAPTER ELEVEN
## BOYS NIGHT OUT

Well, that went great. With a mountain of frustration and anger welling up inside of me, I rode back to Mother Base. After a while, Kyle spoke up. "I can tell you're upset. I didn't exactly know it was a place of worship."

"You lose your morals as soon as an order is placed?" I asked as we reached the base.

Kyle pitched his horse next to mine. "You know I can't deny orders. I'm a soldier. I'm not useful thinking about the people I killed. Are you?"

I stopped and looked back. "No. Hell, I can't talk much, can't I? But I still try to have some reason for it all. Not just because some faceless figure said so."

Kyle placed a hand on my shoulder. "You don't think I hate that too?" He walked away, leaving me to my thoughts.

Over the next week or so Team Foolish was shelved as Miller Corps prepared for the first big push into Godless territory. In that time, I made a new gadget: The extendable blade. I placed it on my left forearm, set to spring out if I squeezed my hand at any time. The blade would extend out at the top, meaning I'd get that extra damage when I punched. Also, Sera came to my tent. We talked. She sometimes stayed the night.

It was night, and we lay together as usual. We always had our space, but we were shoulder to shoulder this time. The same shoulders as that night in Southland...

"Hey, Dopeman?" she said, breaking the silence.

I was half tired, yawning. "Yeah?"

"Do you think I'm pretty?"

"Yeah, of course. You're fine, Sera."

"Then you find me attractive?" She sat up, placing a hand on my chest.

My heart beat faster. "Sera... Where is this coming from?"

"Dopeman." She blushed.

"Sera?" I did the same.

She moved away again, falling asleep eventually. Once I wrapped my arm around her to cuddle, I did the same. She made me feel... special. *What a woman.*

When we woke up the next morning, she didn't comment about our cuddle session, but she did give me a wink and a hug before leaving for the day.

I dawdled away my time outside with my horse, reading a book about a crazy yandere killer.

"See! I knew he'd kill him next!" I yelled after reading the end.

Serena neighed in an argumentative fashion.

"You didn't say that! You said he'd kill the other nerd!"

Another neigh, though rather aggressive.

As I opened my mouth to continue my point, Kyle stepped around the side of the tent. "Were you…"

"Talking to my horse? Yes."

He stared at me.

I stared back.

"Anyways… You, me, and Fisher are going to do a stakeout. Sera will be doing a special op with the scout team."

I nodded and prepared for the trip. One ride later, we camped at a small cliff area that overlooked a fortress.

Kyle pointed at the stone fort patched with mud. "This is Fort Janson, a pre-war fort the United states army used to train young recruits. Now, it's a place of debauchery and anarchy."

Fisher stood and looked at the fort. "Why are we here, eh? I'm sure we're not gonna wait till they're weak or something. This looks to be a major hub for them."

"It is. We've been hitting small hotspots for the last week: hospitals, churches, villages."

"That's part one? You've been hitting places of worship and shelter?" I asked with a hint of annoyance.

"It ruins their morale. This is not a fortress, It's now a major place of worship. The scouting reports say it holds the most precious thing of the Trastorno religion. What that thing is, we'll have to wait and see. Once we spot it, we shoot a flare and watch the fireworks."

Fisher perked up. "Fireworks?"

Kyle smiled. *Scary.*

Fisher and I sat together while Tann lay down opposite us and stared at the night sky.

"So"—I glanced over to Fisher—"You and one of the soldiers…"

He laughed. "Yeah. Of course. She was a monster. She was choking, hitting—"

"Jeez, you alright?"

Fisher nodded and grinned like an idiot. "I was in heaven."

Kyle sat up. "Don't get my soldiers pregnant."

I swiped the air. "Come on, Major. Lighten up. Who was your first?"

"Why would I tell you that? To make conversation?"

"Yes. So, get that stick out of your butt and talk to us."

Tann sighed and hugged his knees. "When I was a recruit, she was named Nat. She invited me to the showers."

Fisher laughed, moving next to Tann. "That story sucked, ya know."

"How? I said what happened."

I moved closer as well. "Where's the setup? The atmosphere? Have you ever even talked to anybody who wasn't not a soldier?"

"No. I haven't had the need to."

"Now you do."

We talked about guy things for the rest of the night. Sorry, boys only!

# CHAPTER TWELVE
## FIREBOMBS AND FORTS

"Hey, Dopeman!" Kyle shook me awake.

It was freezing when I stepped out of the tent. The sun was nowhere in sight, meaning it wasn't past four in the morning. Fisher stepped out while I got my jumpsuit on. "Tann, what the hell?" he complained.

Kyle, the only man who was properly awake, looked back. "This isn't a sleepover. They've brought out the object."

We approached the cliff's edge and looked over. The object was a statue made of pure bronze, in the shape of a tribal man stomping on a mule and elephant. He had on an oversized headdress and loads of tattoos on his body.

"They're really into the lack of government thing, huh?" I said.

Fisher loaded his sniper rifle. "Yeah. Is it just gonna be us three, Tann?"

Kyle shook his head and pulled out a flare gun. "No. I'll shoot this flare here and we'll have air support and about ninety soldiers en route."

"Wait." I walked over to our tent for my shotgun, loading it with regular shells. It was gonna be a long night. "We have working helicopters?"

"Sorta. They work, but not for long distances. We've been prepping them for bombing runs. They fly in, drop the bombs, and leave. At that point, the backup comes in."

It seemed like a nice enough plan. I just hoped it would work. We studied them for a bit.

"Cbaus. Intel says he's their god of chaos. Made to bring down traditional governments and bring 'freedom,' whatever that means." Kyle checked his watch and aimed the flare gun upwards. "It's time."

He pulled the trigger, letting the bright red light fly in the air. We all grabbed our horses and rode downhill and over to the fort. The helicopters roared over our heads, dropping bombs filled with oil. Three was all it took for the fortress to be a glorified oven. The fires were as high as a five-story building, and as we dismounted, the massive horde of the Miller Corps army could be heard in the distance.

Trastornos screamed in pain as they were finished off by the fire. They attempted to run out of the fort, but the fire was persistent, making the pain worse as they fell to the dirt, dragging themselves from the fire.

Fisher started at the chaos. "God, this is—"

"Needed," Kyle finished. "It was needed to start stage two."

"This stage two better be worth it," I said as I petted Serena.

The fire died down as dawn broke. Black char could be seen everywhere, and it smelled awful. Other soldiers made the trip to survey the scene, Sera included, as she had finished her op hours ago.

I held out my arms to embrace her as she came over to survey the damage. "War. This is what war does."

"It's what war did to Dani too, right?" Sera asked.

"Yeah, exactly."

"Dopeman... What happened to Dani?"

# CHAPTER THIRTEEN

## No more dope, man

I sat in my tent with Sera back at Fort Janson.

"Dopeman," Sera said.

I didn't answer. Instead, I twirled a toothpick between my fingers, trying to remember my ex-girlfriend.

"Dopeman! Tell me about Dani!" she yelled.

I snapped out of my trance and slowly turned to face her. "Sera? Why do you want to know about Dani so badly?"

"She was the only woman to make you truly happy, right?"

I started to answer, but I choked on my words. For once, I didn't exactly have the answers. "I... Uh... Yeah, she was."

"What made her so special?"

I looked up, my mind swarmed with memories of the girl with the white hair. "She was the only one who didn't see me as the loser who chose to ruin his life and cripple families with the stuff he sold. I was a human to her."

Sera placed a hand on my shoulder. "You're a human to me..."

"Am I?"

"Of course you are!" Sera gave a reassuring smile.

I wasn't convinced. "Sera, do you like me?"

She nodded slowly. "Yeah, I do."

"Why?"

"You're the best man I've seen in this hell we call the west coast."

I shook my head in disapproval. "I killed aunties and uncles, Sera. I ain't much better."

"But you are!"

"I've killed people that looked like me, poisoned my own kind."

She kept it up. "That's...That's in the past!"

"You're just looking for somebody else to cling to and take care of. You can't be Dani, hon. Sorry."

Tears fell down her face. "You're a real jerk, you know that? Why would you even think I'm trying to—"

I moved to hug her, and she wept in my arms. "I'm scared."

She sniffed. "O-Of what?"

*Of loving again.*

* * *

After the incident on the bridge, we talked more and more. Eventually, I gained feelings for the woman. I took her on a date to an Italian restaurant. She told me about her day, giggling at every joke. Dani couldn't stop looking at me. To be fair, I did the same. I loved to see her little mannerisms, they're what made her so unique.

I swallowed the last of my water, clearly nervous. "Hey," I said as I put the empty glass down.

Dani looked up at me. **"Yeah?"**

"I wanna be your boyfriend."

**"Really? Is that how you ask me?"**

"I-I mean, I practiced all day! I couldn't think of anything to say without sounding dumb. You're perfect. I love the way you look, smell, walk, talk, everything! I can't stop thinking about you and I can't bear living knowing you're not mine!" I stood up, red faced. In hindsight, I was a bit dramatic. However, I still feel those words are true. "I'm in love with you, **Dani Hikari!"**

The whole place turned to see our young-adult drama.

She stood up, grabbed my face, and kissed me deeply. I remember thinking that I would never feel this way again.

A few months later, we started living together. I was smoking and washing the dishes when I felt a flick on the back of my head.

I rubbed my head. "Ow! The hell was that for?"

**"No more selling dope!"** she commanded. She was angry, and started to cry.

I went in to hug her as she repeated the same sentence, letting her...

*Weep.*

"I promise," I muttered as I picked her up. "I won't sell any dope, I promise."

I didn't need a reason. She said it, and it was done. I loved her that much.

I didn't think I ever would love again.

# CHAPTER FOURTEEN

## RADIO DOPEMAN

It was morning. I had sat and held onto Sera the whole night as she cried, and I didn't even notice when she fell asleep on my shoulder. She looked so peaceful... but then again, I could have a biased opinion. I let her down and headed out of the tent into the temporary camp we had made in the charred remains of the fortress after cleaning it out last night. The ground was still scarred black by the flames. It was basically a smaller version of Mother Base. Soldiers had set up a canteen, armory, barracks, and everything needed to serve the basic needs of an army, but I didn't expect us to stay long as it still smelled of burnt flesh. It was haunting, as if the souls of the anarchists still screeched for help.

Kyle Tann, who was talking with another officer, turned to me while coughing. "Morning, Dopeman."

"Hey."

"We got new orders today."

I rolled my eyes. "Ain't that a surprise. Fill me in."

We walked to his tent, and I took a look at the photos scattered on the table. They looked to be shots of some old phone tower. It was rare to even see one standing. The tower was held up with duct tape and prayer. Kyle pointed to the picture. "That is the tower we need. We got intel that about seven years ago during the Intro Wars, an old militia group wanted to restore the phone towers and set up short-range communication around this area to help fight against another extinct group. They didn't have time to finish, as the raging sandstorms and the NRF were gaining strength. They were wiped, and those idiots didn't even take it down. Good for us, because we just figured out how to do that communication trick."

I leaned on the table. I didn't care for a history lesson. "Cut to the chase, Tann. What do I gotta do?"

He tossed me a map, a walkie-talkie, and a small box. The box had a number pad on it, a frequency setter, and a massive mess of wires on the back. "Need you to set this up for us. The process shouldn't be too hard."

Before I could turn to leave, Tann's cold demeanor broke. "Dopeman, I was following orders. They were going to kill us if we didn't do that last night."

I shrugged. "Are you convincing me or yourself?"

Not giving him the chance to answer, I left to start my mission. The tower was still standing, but the metal structure was roped up and falling apart.

"This looks like crap," I mumbled to Serena as I fed her a carrot.

She huffed in agreement.

After dismounting, I climbed the broken metal ladder. With each step I took, the tower groaned to be put out of its misery. Half way up, I felt the tower sway in the wind. A metal peg broke off of it as I continued climbing, making it shake more. Upon reaching the box, I saw another mess of wires. This was gonna take a long time...

After a bit of jerry-rigging and prayer, I finally got the damn thing working. I set it to different frequencies to see if anyone would respond. I started to speak on my hand radio. "Testing, testing. Hellooo?"

"This Major Kyle Tann, over. We hear you, Dopeman."

I smiled to myself. We could finally talk without sending letters, at least in this small area. "Good, so now I can—"

A large boom interrupted my thoughts. "Kyle! Mayday! One of the camps to the west just got bombed!"

"Wait, what?! Get to the camp immediately! We'll meet you there!"

In the background Tann yelled for someone to mobilize. I hurried down to Serena and we raced down to the camp.

I reached the camp before Tann and saw that the situation was worse than I could have imagined. Men were writhing in pain, their flesh burning away. The powder looked to be acidic to the touch. I'd never seen a weapon like this before. The sound of hooves hitting sand could be heard in the distance.

Kyle and his men rode up to me. "Angel Waste. Think of it as white phosphorus on steroids. We don't know who made it. We fought against it ourselves during the Intro Wars. It's not a pretty sight. The only people who used it were the NRF..." Something clicked in his mind. "Don't tell me the NRF is working with the—"

A burning soldier crawled up to us, shaking in pain. Before we could do anything, another sudden pop went off, and we saw the white ball in the air. All the horses and soldiers ran with me, but not Tann. Tann carried the man out of the danger zone and threw him before the bomb hit. The Angel Waste hit the earth and a massive spread of white billowed over the ground. The world vibrated as I dove for safety, hands over my head. When the blast settled, we looked up to see the burned soldier motionless, and Kyle was yelling in agony. His left arm was burned and the flesh was falling off. I ran to his side, picking him up while the others grabbed the other injured soldier.

*Why did I agree to this?*

# CHAPTER FIFTEEN
## PHANTOM PAIN

I brought Tann to a tent back at Fort Janson; there was no way we could get to Mother Base in time. I held him down as the doctors tried to examine his arm.

"How bad is it?" I asked, as Kyle writhed in pain.

The doc shook his head. "We're going to have to—"

"Nooo!" Kyle roared. "You're not going to cut it! No!"

"It's that or die, Major! We can't save it! Even if we get to Mother Base, it's too late!" the doctor yelled back.

Tann was panicking even more, attempting to get up from the table. I'd had enough. I smacked his face. "Kyle, you damn fool. These people need you! You're a soldier, act like it!"

He gritted his teeth and took a few short breaths. "Towel. Towel and water."

Without hesitation, I got what he asked for and helped him brace himself for amputation. When it was all done, I left the tent to calm myself. Fisher and Sera came up to me as I sat next to my tent, entertaining Serena.

"Hey, dude," Fisher said.

Sera kneeled next to me. "You okay, Dopeman?"

I nodded. "I'm just here. Tann is still alive, but the things I saw at that camp were—"

"It's all good." Fisher waved his hand, signaling me not to elaborate. "We're just making sure you're okay." Fisher checked his watch. "Well, I got myself a date with a beautiful muscular woman. I'll be seeing you."

I scoffed. "You better be ready for the missions tomorrow!"

"No promises!"

We laughed as Fisher walked away.

"You wanna talk?" I asked.

She nodded, and we stepped into my tent.

I sat and grabbed some water. I needed a distraction. "I'm gonna ask you a bunch of questions, okay?"

Sera smiled. "Sounds like fun."

"Hobbies?"

"Reading, horseback riding, and shooting."

"Favorite color?"

"Blue."

"Why do you have such a massive gun?"

"Well, I wanted to prove some guy wrong during a shooting competition. I won, and I kept his gun."

I paused. I liked her smile and the way she talked. This feeling was something I hadn't felt in a long time. The way she moved, the way she cared about me so much... She wanted to latch onto me. Maybe she really did care about me. Maybe she really meant what she said—Sera liked me. I stared at her for a while.

Sera blushed. "What's your next question?" She tilted her head, playing with the hem of her dress.

I took a chance. "You ever been kissed?"

She stopped moving. Her pale cheeks flushed pink. "No..."

I scooted closer, ready for the next step. "Did you want to change that?"

Sera grabbed my dirty shirt and pulled me close. We locked lips for a few moments. Then we pulled away.

"Nice," I said, still thinking about her soft lips.

"That's all you have to say?"

"It was nice, wasn't it?"

Sera giggled. "Fool."

I stopped by the medical tent the next day to see Kyle sitting outside on an old oil drum with a bandage on what was left of his arm. He shoved a couple of painkillers in his mouth and washed them down with water before brushing past to his own tent. I followed, stopping just on the other side of the tent flap.

"Kyle?"

"What?" He was frustrated. It was obvious why.

"You could always get a prosthetic. Those prototype robot arms are still working on—"

"That's not the point!" He threw a few books off his makeshift desk. "I followed orders. All I do is the right thing. I don't drink, smoke, party, have constant sex—nothing! I get hurt, and what do I get? NOTHING! " He hit the desk with his hand. "How is that fair, Dopeman? How is that fair?"

I walked in, exhaling softly. "In my eyes, we get hurt to learn something or get stronger. I can't say to the pain you're feeling, but I can say you're not alone, Kyle. You have people here for you."

"Sure as hell doesn't feel that way. I have the entire operation on my shoulders, and I don't even get a thank you from the higher-ups. All I do is follow orders."

"Then do it your way."

He scoffed. "My way?"

I patted him on the shoulder. "You'll figure it out once you do a mission the way that you *want*, not the way that you're *told*."

Kyle grunted, calming down. "You know, I still feel my arm. The sensation of what was once lost. The phantom pain."

"Yeah. It sucks, I know. You'll get a cooler arm and you'll look sick!"

Tann laughed and leaned on the desk. "I guess..."

He wasn't a bad dude; he was a victim of war.

# CHAPTER SIXTEEN
## LOOKOUT: WATCHING ANGELS SING

"Hey…"

"Huh? Where am I?"

**"Do you like her?"**

"D-Dani?"

**"Answer my question."**

"Yes, I do."

**"Then why do you still think of me?"**

"What do you mean?"

**"Let go."**

"Dani, you're not making sense."

**"Let go. Let go. Let go."**

* * *

Another long night. I felt guilty. Sera didn't deserve this turmoil. She had unofficially moved into my tent. She latched on to me for dear life when we slept. Sera had that understanding only the best people have. I liked how much she held on to me; it felt so familiar. She was so beautiful, like…

I couldn't think about her. I couldn't.

I walked out to see the troops in lukewarm spirits as they saw Kyle walk around. He'd recovered in a matter of days and was helping me out with a new operation to get rid of the Angel Waste. I called it Operation: Wing Clipper. With the task force set up, all we needed was to scope out the battlefield and get a map set up. For now, I got the news that communication across southern Nevada was set up. One of the soldiers told me that a woman from Badland was attempting to call me. Well, who could guess that?

I went to the radio and turned on the mic. "Harper?"

Some static, then I heard a voice. "Yeah? Dopeman! Finally!"

"How did you know I was even at camp?"

"Well, I heard that Miller Corps had set up a radio in town. I convinced them to have me test it out. I called the main base, and one of my connections told me you were here."

"Slick. So how are you? You got my letter?"

Harper laughed. "Yeah. I'm happy that you even remembered to send me a letter back."

"You're a good friend, Harper. I like talking to you."

She started sniffling. The connection worsened. "You... W-well, I can't wait till you get back! I'm sure you have a ton of stories to tell! We're getting rumors of your exploits in the war, and people can't wait for more."

"Like Dopeman, or like Foolish Courier?"

"At this point, it's about half and half."

"Good. Well, I got more work to do, keep spreading your good name! Stay safe!"

"You too, Dopeman!"

As soon as the moon rose, the scouting party was on. We organized into teams of two, with me teaming up with Fisher. We rode to the field and took position among the tall rocks. Fisher pulled out a recorder for note-taking purposes.

"This is Dopeman. Date is November 2nd, 2092, 12:50 AM. I see"—I zoomed in with my binoculars—"five catapults. They are too far apart for a bombing run. We may have to go on foot to destroy them. Next to the catapults are tons of Angel Waste." I pull out a camera to take a picture of the placements and the waste. "I also see some freedom men." I took a picture of them. "I also... Crap."

Fisher looked up. "What? No..."

"It's NRF. NRF is working with Tribe Trastorno. It's confirmed now."

They were supplying them with men and gear. I had to take a few more pictures of the men together. The NRF usually wore riot gear. They had their large shield logo on the shoulder of their uniforms, making sure we knew what they were. Once we got the shots, we rode out.

"So," Fisher said when we were about at the fort, "what now?"

I laughed. "We just kill them too."

# CHAPTER SEVENTEEN
## OPERATION: WING CLIPPER

**Operation:** Wing Clipper

**Date:** November 5th, 2092

**Location:** Godless Territory, Nevada. Southern Region

**Task Force Leader:** Major Kyle Tann

**Objective:** Eliminate the Angel Waste held by the NRF, destroy the catapults, and eliminate any force that stands in the way of this objective.

The location is set up on top of a hill and mostly surrounded by rocks, allowing no flank operation from the back. Area is heavily guarded by Tribe Trastorno and NRF, making a stealth op mission close to impossible. The only course of attack is to directly strike or hit the side.

This attack will be split into two teams. Team A will be outfitted with hazmat suits to resist the Angel Waste. They will directly strike the catapults. Team B will then enter from the side approximately two minutes after Team A. Due to the low number of suits, Team B will only have gas masks. Team B will be in charge of disarming the catapults and Angel Waste, and destroying them.

God save us,

Maj. Kyle Tann, Miller Corps.

* * *

I was in a carriage with my team and Kyle. Despite only recently recovering from his last run-in with Angel Waste, he insisted on tagging along. After all, he did direct this entire operation.

"We know what to do?" I said, looking at my squad.

Sera and Fisher nodded, ready to fight.

As the dossier said, we came in late and unprotected. We fitted our gas masks as we entered a white mist—Angel Waste—dispersed through the air. All I could see was the muzzle flash of gunfire. I heard screaming, and the smell of burnt flesh infiltrated my nostril. My skin began to itch and burn, and I felt sorry for the horses breathing it in. As we reached the side and Team B's three wagons started to advance, the plan was quickly halted by an Angel Waste blast from a catapult. The wagon in front of us got hit, and the shockwave rolled over us, sending our horses flying. Unable to withstand the impact, the wagon splintered and broke.

Fisher dragged me out of the mess.

Sera kneeled to check on me. "Dopeman?"

I looked at the white haze around us, my ears ringing. I started to panic.

Struggling to breathe, my eyes rapidly darted around, trying to make sense of what just happened. I crawled to make the world stop spinning.

Kyle hit my mask. "Let's move! You're a soldier now, act like one!"

I was still shaken, but I got up with my team and we followed the pistol-toting Major. Kyle ran to waction. I leaped over a rock, popping an NRF guy in the chest. I got behind cover to shoot at the three guys guarding the catapult. With the lack of visibility and the damage on the armor of the tribesmen, the waste must've spilled and spread throughout the battle. I ran over to the first catapult I saw while Sera and Fisher laid down cover fire. As I started to set up my charged explosive, one of the tribesmen charged his shoulder to my gut, spearing me. His skin was basically ruined. He pulled a knife from his belt and lunged for my chest. Lucky for me, I had my arm blade. I squeezed my palm to unleash the blade, sliced off the man's arm as he tried to attack me, stabbed him in the leg to have him on his knees, and went for a deep cut at his throat. I kicked off the freedom man and continued my mission.

When I finished setting up the bomb, I radioed the Major. "Kyle, this is Dopeman. Got my charge down."

Kyle picked up. I heard heavy gunfire in the background. "Dopeman! We have a problem. The last location we need is covered by a man with a minigun."

"What?! How the hell did the NRF get that much tech?"

"We don't know! We need him gone!" The radio went dead. Damn.

I ran back to my team. "Ok! Dude with a minigun, I got a plan. You two distract him, okay?"

Fisher shrugged. "What are you planning?"

Sera scoffed. "Like he'd tell us. We don't have time, my skin burns, let's just do it!"

We split up. I ran to take some gloves off a dead NRF soldier. They had just enough padding to make this work. I grabbed a ball of Angel Waste. This was a dumb idea. I ran back to my team. They were surprised I had a ball of toxic waste, but they followed my lead and ran to distract the guy, taking random shots to keep him guessing where the enemy was located. I got close enough, and made my move.

"Snowball fight!" I yelled, chucking the waste at the minigun man. As he disintegrated and the army moved on to the last bomb. I removed what was left of the gloves. My hands were in bad shape—not cut them off bad, but pretty bad.

Kyle stopped to look at my hands. "Let's hurry before they get worse."

We ran away, past the corpses of our horses and some unlucky soldiers. Once we got to a safe distance, Kyle set off the bombs, sending it all sky high.

The waste was gone, but it wasn't exactly destroyed. Some of it lingered; as the wind picked up, it would blow further south. "That doesn't look good," I mumbled. My hands were shaking, my skin was burned and boiled.

Kyle shook his head. "What are we fighting for?"

"You ask that now? You seemed so confident before."

"After you have a kid to come back to, dying for democracy doesn't sound as great as it used to."

# CHAPTER EIGHTEEN
## RESTING IN, COMING OUT

The operation was a moderate success, but we lost quite a few people on Team A. Those hazmat suits only did so much to protect against direct blasts. Team B didn't lose anyone, but all of us were put in medical care due to burns. I also had to treat my hands for touching that Angel Waste. For the next few weeks, I was relaxing with the team, making sure I was recovering. I couldn't use my hands a lot, so I had Sera help me with minor tasks.

I was in my tent one day, relaxing. Fisher walked in. "I wanna talk to ya about something."

I sit up. "And that is?"

"I'll be blunt. I think I might be in love."

"Oh? With that woman?"

"About that..." He scratched the back of his head. "She's a he."

"A man?" I asked, curious.

"Yeah. Fun fact about me is that Fisher isn't really my real name. I used to be a fisherman, so the name kinda stuck. Before the war, I was Samuel. And when you're fishing with big dudes for months at a time, you gain... interests."

"It's a cool name, Sam. You had to be on the east coast, yeah? Why did you even lie in the first place?"

"So," Fisher started, "we went fishing off the coast of Boston. It was just me and this guy, his name was Wendall. We fished there, but some huge storm washed us off course, leaving us without enough gas to return home. We were stranded for about three months."

"Three months?!"

"It was a freak storm, nothing but rain and wind for ninety days. I was with Wendall, so we ate together, fished together, slept together..." He smiled to himself. "I felt like I knew everything about him in those weeks. Eventually, admiration turned to lust. I wanted him and he wanted me. And you guessed it, he was strong."

"So, you like 'em both, yeah?"

"Yup. Pretty much."

"So, what happened to Wendall?"

He sighed, fishing for a cigarette. "When we got picked up, he told me not to mention this. He told me to forget everything. I was told to pretend he didn't love me. How much he loved me. How we made love. It was the most emotional time of my life, and I was supposed to..." He shook his head. I wrapped an arm around his shoulders to comfort him. Fisher continued. "I felt shame for my feelings, so I went for the next best thing."

"That being the women you like now."

Fisher nodded.

"Well, I'm okay with it. You go tell your soldier how you feel. This time he won't leave. I'm sure of it."

He kissed my cheek. "Thanks, Dopeman. If you were single and like a little more swole I would easily date you." He stood.

I realized what he said. "Wait, single? I am—" I stopped.

Fisher turned and smiled. "See? You and Sera are perfect for each other. Enjoy yourselves."

I rubbed my face. God, I hated feelings so much.

Later that day, I went to Kyle's tent to check on him. He wore bandages from the neck down, like me. "The General sent his personal regards on the mission, Dopeman."

I nodded. "Wow. That's rad, Kyle. I didn't know I'm gaining traction here."

"I suppose it is. Not every day an outsider gets a nod from the General. I'm also a Colonel now."

I threw my hands in the air, smiling. "Woah! That's cool, bro. I'm happy. Congrats."

Kyle cracked a smile. "I'll celebrate when the war is over. For now, we got a mission from the top brass."

"What's the deal?"

He opened a map of southern Nevada. "To discover the new problem we made. Experts are calling it False Heaven."

"False Heaven?"

"Yeah. The land of Angel Waste."

# CHAPTER NINETEEN
## BATTLE OF LAST CHANCE, PART ONE

False Heaven: Land near the border of Arizona covered by Angel Waste. It seemed, from the reports so far, that it was only a matter of time before it blew further south throughout the rest of Arizona. It also seemed that we'd pushed the Trastornos further out of Nevada. The men on the frontlines did a good job, and we were just about ready to make a final push. There were a few problems, however. In order to focus on finishing the tribe, we'd have to let False Heaven fester until we fully pushed Trastorno out of the fight.

The tribe was apparently making camp in a town that bordered False Heaven, called Last Chance. Miller Corps was going to invade in wagons, with Kyle and I riding in a single helicopter to oversee the battle.

Before I stepped on, Kyle grabbed my shoulder. "Dopeman, I have something for you." He handed me a brand new TK-17. It was a shiny submachine gun. He handed me a few clips as well. I smiled as I applied the strap and hung it on the opposite side of my shotgun. "Thanks, Kyle."

I gave the one-armed man a hug. He accepted it.

I stepped into the flying rust bucket and sat down, looking at the army getting ready to fight. "Hey!" I yelled.

They all stopped to look at me.

"We're almost home for Thanksgiving, boys. Just remember that!"

I got smiles and a few claps. Then we were off. The wagons clattered away. We rose in the air and got a good look at the massive army that had been sent for this push.

I looked over to Tann. "We got this, Colonel."

He nodded in response. "We damn well better."

As we reached Last Chance, we saw a massive wall of white. It was like a gate of clouds. They called it False Heaven for a reason. It was a beautiful sight to see. I couldn't see for long, however. The battle started with the tribe shooting at the helicopter. It didn't help that this rust trap couldn't handle anything. The pilot lost control quickly. We weren't that high, so it wasn't too rough of a crash landing. We smacked down into the sand and rolled a few times before the helicopter screeched to a halt. I was shellshocked, dazed, and confused as I climbed out. I saw Kyle dragging the pilot from the wreckage. She had a piece of shrapnel protruding from her leg. She was screaming; asking if she was going to lose her leg, begging for help. I ran over.

Kyle waved me off. "I got this. Help the men with the battle."

I nodded and ran, SMG ready for violence. My forehead was bleeding but whatever. Disregarding the pain, I ran up a sandhill to see a warzone. There were bodies strewn about everywhere, explosions rocking the ground, cries of pain and death. When suddenly, I heard something I thought I'd never hear in a million years, ever again.

Thunder.

The walls of False Heaven broke and a cloud floated overhead. I shot the last tribesman I could see, then ran to Sera, who was popping at fools with a DMR.

I slid over to her in cover as the cloud blocked out the sun. "You see that?" I yelled, pointing at it. "Where's Fisher?"

She shot twice and ducked back behind cover. "I don't know! I think Fisher is in the city with the other half of the army!"

The thunder boomed, shaking us to the core and lightning flashed, striking the ground nearby. Rain fell—well, I say rain when I should say little drops of Angel Waste—like a light sprinkle, but it still hurt. We had to push in.

"Charge!" I shouted as I ran forward with my shotgun.

I loaded in Demon's Kiss and hopped over the line, getting a shot in the left shoulder that I'd definitely feel later. I opened fire, letting Tribe Trastorno feel the kiss of flame and ducked into a run-down restaurant for cover as the rest of the army came in behind me to clean house.

Sera chased after me. "God, Dopeman! Your shoulder!"

It was bleeding badly. I shook my head. "I need to find Fisher."

"No, you don't!"

I didn't look at her, I simply tried to radio Fisher. "Team Foolish. Come in, this is Dopeman."

Static.

I loaded my regular shells as I stepped onto the window frame, ready to go.

"Dopeman…" She stepped up behind me. "Please, rest. We can't go out, the rain is getting worse!"

I turned and let a tear fall down my slightly burned face. "I can't forgive myself if somebody else dies because of me." I lifted my mask and kissed her, before heading into the rain.

*I'm sorry, Sera.*

It's not your fault I can't move on.

# CHAPTER TWENTY
## BATTLE OF LAST CHANCE, PART TWO

*You didn't save her.*

*You watched her bleed out, and she got one last look at you.*

*Your final view of her is a shot to the throat, her life draining from her face.*

*You want that?*

*You want to see that again?*

The rain was getting worse. The ground sizzled as I sprinted from house to house, trying to avoid as much as I could.

"Dopeman! Come in, Dopeman! Downtown isn't safe. We have to evacuate now. The rain will intensify, it's already unsafe to even be where you are right now!" Kyle called out from my radio.

I picked it up and responded, "That's all the more reason to hurry. Dopeman out."

I didn't need more reminders of my mistake—I was committed now.

* * *

I turned off the television. I didn't need more reminders of my mistake.

"**Crack cocaine**, commonly known simply as **crack**, and also known as **dope**, is a free base form of cocaine that can be smoked. Crack offers a short, intense high to smokers. The Manual of Adolescent Substance Abuse Treatment calls it the most **addictive** form of cocaine."

"The crack epidemic claims another life in San Francisco. He was only twenty-one—"

"Crack deal goes wrong in downtown San Francisco, leaving three dead."

* * *

I didn't have time to be safe. I ignored the burning pain and ran across the mud brick bridge that gapped the residential area to downtown. It was chaos. Lightning struck an old theater, illuminating the mass of people. Trastorno was slaughtering Miller Corps. They had a better tolerance of the pain of the Angel Waste-infused rain. I had to help. I ran toward the action, loading my regular slugs. I ignored my skin, the scream of nerves as they were exposed to the air. Then again, all I'd ever done was ignore.

* * *

All I'd ever done was ignore.

"Crack first saw widespread use as a recreational drug in primarily impoverished neighborhoods in New York City, Philadelphia, Baltimore, Washington, D.C., Los Angeles, **San Francisco**, and Miami..."

"My baby was too young! He was gonna be a basketball player, he was already in the draft!"

"It's been a problem for a while. It's just a lot of dealers around here. It's a profitable market."

* * *

I charged into the fight, shooting the first guy I saw in the head. The rest of the tribe saw me and tried to get revenge. I dodged, but I couldn't properly roll into cover, and a bullet grazed my left ankle. I yelled in pain, but I had to push on. I got my SMG and shot the two guys charging at me. I shot three more before reloading. As I got my clip in, a man with a large machete slashed at me. The machete cut through my jacket and shirt, piercing the skin over my ribs. I rolled out of the way I made my arm blade appear and sent it right in his throat. Then I stood. Miller Corps was regaining momentum. Good. Before I could celebrate, lightning struck the tree next to me. Thunder crashed and shook the ground, and I fell again. The combination of my blood loss and the pain from the rain was too much. I held my side as I crawled into a nearby house, looking at the battle through a window. My vision was blurring.

* * *

"Reports are saying out of the forty-five percent of Americans addicted to crack cocaine, fifteen percent come from San Francisco alone."

"It's bad out here, man. These kids gotta go home to their dads and moms on that stuff."

"I can't believe that these people that look like us can just sell this. You ruined our community for years, for what?"

* * *

Yeah, for what?

I couldn't see much…

A man with a familiar face walked inside…

"Dopeman!" he cried.

It was Fisher—the man I was trying to save.

Was I going to fail? **Again?**

# CHAPTER TWENTY-ONE
## WHITE TO RED

Summer.

*Man, do I miss the Old World...*

I woke up pretty excited. Ever since I got together with Dani, I quit dealing drugs, quit smoking, and sold my expensive apartment to live in a modest home. With a new start in mind, I wanted to propose.

June 22nd was payday. My mundane job as a cashier had netted me a decent bit of cash. Dani worked as a nurse, so she was usually gone most of the night and morning. I got up, got dressed, and made my way to the train station.

The hypertrain was generally peaceful. I got to stand and watch the train speed towards my destination. Relaxing against a window, I relaxed and enjoyed the gentle sway of the train. Mounted TVs played the news, which I normally blocked out, but today was different—I heard something I couldn't ignore.

"Let's hope Germany isn't serious. In local news, the crack epidemic claims another life in San Francisco. Twenty-one-year-old Fortis Kay was a talented basketball player with dreams of getting into the league. Now he can never achieve that."

*No. No...*

"His mother, Ava Kay, was devastated by the loss of her son."

"My baby was too young! He was gonna be a basketball player, he was already in the draft!"

Thankfully, the train stopped at the station. Once the doors opened, I ran to the bathroom to throw up. I couldn't breathe as the cries echoed in my head. Dizziness washed over me and I knew I had to call Dani.

**"Hello?"** She picked up.

I was panting, struggling to catch my breath. "Dani... I'm freaking out."

**"Hey, hey. Where are you?"**

"Downtown... Train station... Bathroom... Please..." I slid down the wall, hugging my knees.

*There is no redemption for me. I can't come back from this.*

*I can't. I just can't!*

**"Hey!"** Dani was there, tapping my shoulder. **"That was the past. You're not the Dopeman anymore, okay?"**

I must've been speaking out loud. How long had I been like this?

I nodded slowly.

**"I can see why you feel guilty. I've seen so many patients overdose regardless of my efforts to help them kick the habit. It's a cruel world, and you had your hand in it. Do you know what you can do? If you messed something up, fix it. Make this city better. I know you can."**

I looked up, tears in my eyes. "I love you."

**"I love you too."** She moved in to kiss me. As we kissed, we heard the alarm go off. THE alarm. The one signaling that America actually done it. They had nuked Germany.

I stood up and grabbed her hand. "We gotta go, now!" It was only a matter of time before retaliation. We had no time to head back home, so we ran across downtown, looking for anything to use as cover. We pushed through the panicked crowd and saw an old man walking into an alleyway. We followed.

"Hey, old man!" I yelled.

He turned and shook his head. "No! I found this here bunker. It's mine!"

Dani walked up from behind and clasped her hands together. **"Please! We need to find shelter, sir!"**

The old man was pondering, but it was too late. We felt the rumble of the nuke dropping from miles away. We ran into the bunker and closed it.

"Damn it," the old man said as he sat in his chair to sulk.

"Thanks," I responded sarcastically.

For the next six months, we sat dormant in the bunker, making sure we could do whatever we needed to survive. I found an old shotgun and taught myself how to tinker. The old man was a gun nut, so he taught me all he could. When I had finished modifying the gun, Dani carved her name into the buttstock. I proposed there, and she accepted.

Soon after, the old man died. He went peacefully, but it still left us in a bunker with a dead man. I didn't know what to do. As I sat in bed messing with my gun and loading five shells, Dani sat on the floor, staring at the body across from us. She'd covered him in a blanket the day before.

**"Hey. What are we going to do when he decomposes?"**

I haven't thought of that. "We... We could burn him. Like the Vikings."

She sighed. **"We need to get him out of this bunker, and we can't keep living like this forever."**

"I'd rather deal with this than go out there. You don't know what creature or ungodly being is out there."

**"I'd say we got a month till the food runs out. Then what? We go out there hungry and not fit enough to face whatever challenge is out there?"**

I looked back to my gun. I didn't want anything to happen to Dani, of course. I was more worried about her being alone because of my death, or even worse...I was so wrapped up in thought I didn't notice her standing to kiss me. **"Trust your wife. She can handle herself. I love you so much."**

I kissed her back, holding her head to sink in the passionate smooch. "I love you too. We'll... We'll go outside, okay?"

With that, I got on my old pre-war boots and walked over to the button to release the hatch. I hovered over it, looking at Dani. She wore a pistol that I had given her, with a few clips on her hip. I sighed nervously and pressed the button, opening the bunker for the first time in six months.

The doors opened to... sand? A sandstorm? In San Francisco? We looked at each other in confusion as we walked up the stairs, using our hands mostly as cover as the storm raged. Blood-red clouds surged with lightning.. As we left the alley, Dani and I saw the torn streets, fallen cables, and rubble from buildings; a disaster with a sprinkle of sand to make it extra special.

I thought of turning back, but we had to figure out if there were any survivors. Under the cover of the howling wind and threatening thunder, we made our way past the dilapidated buildings and rotting corpses, all covered by this mysterious sand. We searched about six blocks of downtown before we saw signs of life, and the sign we saw was a bad one.

Four people wearing baggy jeans and chest plates cut from car hoods were on the verge of killing their fellow man who lay in an alley with stab wounds all over his body. He was begging for mercy as they laughed. I had seen enough. I wanted to go, but Dani watched with a look in her eye I hadn't seen before. She aimed her pistol and fired on instinct. The shot knocked her back and I had to catch her, but the bullet lodged in the side of his neck. As the raider fell to the sandy street, blood oozing from his throat, the remaining three turned to face us. Dani was shaking. She had just taken a life, and shock set in at the worst time. I grabbed her arm and ran as the raiders sprinted after us. Once we reached the entrance of the alleyway, I aimed my gun at the approaching raiders. I saw shadows and shot, hitting one in the chest, killing him. It didn't stop another from tackling me to the ground. He tried to hit me, but I blocked his attempt and whacked him in the jaw with the butt of my gun. I blew his head off, blood and brains littering the sandy concrete. I stood up and turned my head to see...

Dani, with a knife in her chest. I shot the remaining raider in the chest, and continued shooting until I ran out of ammo. I crawled over to my wife and held her in my arms.

"No. No, no, no, no, no..." I mumbled to myself. I picked her body up and ran, barely making it back to the bunker without dropping her. Closing the door, I collapsed to the floor, holding her yet again.

Dani was in shock. She was crying, most likely due to the pain or the fear of death. It didn't matter much anymore.

"Dani, Dani. Don't... I... No..." I sobbed.

She put a hand on my face, a final gesture as she faded from this world.

"Dani... Please..." I said, hugging her dead body as I cried in her chest. I was a mess, cursing whoever I could, blaming everybody I could. Even myself. All I could say was...

*Goodbye, Dani.*

# CHAPTER TWENTY-TWO
## ESCAPE FROM FALSE HEAVEN

My eyes opened slowly. As I stirred, I felt a sharp pain in my side. I looked down to see my wound bandaged. As my hearing recovered, I heard the constant wind and thunder. I looked around. I was in some shack made of sandstone. The floor was old broken wood with barricaded windows, sheltering me from the dangers outside. I hopped off the makeshift cot, slowly got my clothes back on, and made sure all my guns were loaded. As I re-armed, a man in a hazmat suit burst in. I aimed my shotgun and he put his hands up, "Stop! It's Fisher!" he yelled.

He sounded tired as he shut the door, pulling another suit out from behind him. I set the shotgun down, sighing. "Oh man, you alright? Where are we?"

He threw me the suit. "False Heaven. We're still in town. The walls fell, and it's some kind of mix of the sandstorm and Angel Waste."

"So that's False Heaven," I said, pulling my suit on. "A place where the storms never stop."

"Exactly. However, there's a different reason that I wanted the hazmat gear on."

I sat down, familiarizing myself with the suit's overlays. It was good tech. It told you your heart rate, weather conditions, and threat outlines. "Why's that, Sam?"

"Well, when I was running for the suits, I held my breath because it felt weird to breathe. It didn't feel harmful at all."

"Huh. That's odd. Where's the rest of the army?"

Fisher shook his head. "Gone. We're the last two alive from the battle. Being in here makes the reception garbage as well."

"So, we just walk out of here? Do we even got a map?"

Fisher pulls out the Miller Corps map with his personalized markings of Mother Base, False Heaven, and the surrounding area. "If we keep walking east, we should be fine."

We opened the doors, heading outside. The sky looked like a freakish, white eye. It reminded me of the red sky from the Intro Wars. The sandstorm was almost like a snowstorm, dusting the ground with a coarse powder. Limped slightly, I saw skeletons where there should have been fresh corpses.

We headed out of town and crested a dune. Before us was a horde of people walking, rotting away. Tons of mindless drones, blocking the way out. I aimed my SMG at the crowd. "Are those..."

"Zombies?" Fisher finished for me. "Sure looks like it. I knew we couldn't breathe this crap in."

"Well," I loaded my last high explosive slug and nodded to myself. "Let's rock."

"You sure? Your side still needs plenty of time to heal. I didn't even properly—"

I didn't let Fisher finish. I slid down from the dune, shooting the slug, causing a knot of zombies to explode. The horde began to turn. Fisher slid after me, handguns blazing. I switched to my SMG and started shooting before they could get their hands on me. Fisher was behind, taking shits at everything that moved.

The horde seemed endless. Sizzling semi-corpses swinging desiccated limbs, though strangely, they didn't want to bite us. It seemed like they wanted to beat me to death. Running out of options, I pulled out my arm blade and started hacking. It made things faster, but eventually, the bastards got a hit on my helmet. It cracked, causing me to yell and lash out even more. Fisher saw what had happened and pushed me forward, through the horde and over the sand, until we came up to the edge of the boiling cloud that marked False Heaven. Removing my helmet, I looked at the bright, blue sky and felt the heat. I turned for Fisher, grabbing him and pulling him out. We could finally breathe. It was over.

I pulled out my radio. "Kyle, come in. This is Dopeman."

Static, then a voice. "Dopeman? Are you with Fisher?"

"Yeah."

"We'll be taking you home soon," Kyle said.

*They'd better.*

# CHAPTER TWENTY-THREE
## FIGURE IT OUT, DOPEMAN

I went back to my tent to relax, but it wasn't long before Sera came in. She sat on the floor, opposite my bed. She wouldn't speak.

After about thirty minutes, I had to say something. "I'm sorry."

She scoffed. " You said you wouldn't do that anymore. What's your deal? You think you were the only drug dealer?"

I shook my head slowly. "I…"

"No! You weren't. You didn't ruin the city by yourself. Hell, that world is dead and gone, Dopeman!"

"That doesn't have to do with anything, okay? I just wanted to save Fisher."

"By killing yourself in the process?!"

I stood up, upset. "Better than leaving him to hang!"

She did the same. "Your luck is going to run out. Look at you! You look beaten all over!"

"It's fine, okay? Why are you on my back so much? Why do you care?!"

Her eyes welled up with tears. "I don't want to lose you! I don't want to lose another person I care about!"

I sighed. "Look, I…"

A soldier lifted the tent flap. "Dopeman, Major Tann needs you."

Kyle had certainly changed in the span of a few days. He wore a nice red beret with his usual army attire. He also had a scarf around his neck. The most important thing was his new metal arm. It was silver, shiny. He turned to face me. "Dopeman. Do I look cool?"

"Hell yeah!" I yelled, sitting on the desk. "You look nice, man. Like the arm?"

He played with it, adjusting the fingers, twisting the hand. "Yes. While my old hand still bugs me, this works well. I can finally use a rifle at the very least."

I laughed. "Good, you can be the best on the battlefield again. So, what's the deal?"

Kyle pulled out a makeshift map and circled False Heaven. "It wasn't mentioned in your report, but are there zombies in False Heaven? Or…"

"There are, but they're basically mindless drones."

Kyle nodded. "Well, that's not good. That's why we got these orders." He pointed to the north, near Flagstaff, Arizona. "NRF territories. The general ordered us to stay off the front lines, so the tribe fight is done for us."

"What are our orders, then?"

"We head into Arizona and figure out exactly what False Heaven is and how it came to be. If anyone knows about the properties of Angel Waste, it's them."

I looked at the map. "Heard this place sucks. Full of Desert Demons."

"Yup. Better get ready. We leave tomorrow."

# CHAPTER TWENTY-FOUR
## ON THE ROAD TO ARIZONA

I was in the tent with Sera, thinking of what to do next. She hadn't said a word, hadn't even looked at me since I stepped back in a few minutes before. I had to say something to ease the tension, but I was scared of what was on her mind. Was she having second thoughts? Did she hate me? Then again, I should be thinking of myself really. I couldn't shake my feelings for Dani. Every time we slept together, I had flashes of the one I used to cherish. It was a hard feeling to get rid of. Maybe I didn't want to get rid of it at all. I looked at her, hugging her knees across from me. I opened my mouth to say something, but she put a finger in the air.

"Let me tell you a story," she said.

I nodded.

"I was always in a position of caring. I cared for my parents when they were sick, I cared for my sister when she was a kid. I was always... caring. When the bombs dropped, I didn't even know where my sister went. She'd gone to another person's bunker, but I was so terrified that I'd lost her. I needed somebody to protect."

I looked down. "I thought you lost everyone."

"Yeah, I did. I sent her off to the east coast when I found her again. Since so many people wanted to be on the east to avoid the Miller Corps-NRF nonsense, there wasn't enough space for both of us on the convoy to Virginia, and the NUSA government had a stronger presence there than in the wild west. I got stronger, using my farmhand skills to help a community in northern Nevada. It was there I met Dorian, and I found another person to take care of."

"Then he died, and then you found me. I figured, so what's the deal? Do you see me as some kid, or someone you actually like?"

"I like you, Dopeman. Don't be like that. I do like you."

I sighed. "Yeah, I know. Thank you for telling me, Sera."

"Yeah..."

I moved closer to hold her hand. She squeezed back. I leaned in to kiss her cheek; she turned her head and kissed my lips.

*Please, let go.*

I snapped back, laughing nervously. "Let's sleep. We gotta go to Arizona tomorrow."

She looked concerned, but she knew she wasn't gonna get an answer from me. "All right..."

After an awkward sleep with my strong person of interest, we woke up and got dressed to grab the newly repaired helicopters, now upgraded for long-range travel. I would have to leave Serana behind for this trip, sadly. One of the soldiers would bring her to Harper for safekeeping. I kissed my horse on the forehead and got in the helicopter. The colonel stepped in with my team, and off we went.

Sitting on the cold metal, looking at the sand below, was calming. For once I felt like I could reflect.

I felt exhausted. I was tired of just about everything. I'd been shot and stabbed, with about a week to recover before I had to get back up. I honestly didn't know how much I had left in the tank, but I needed to keep pushing for my team—I couldn't let Kyle down. I sat by the helicopter window, looking out at the sand dunes and destroyed buildings. It was a constant reminder of what happens when you engage in war.

Kyle cleared his throat. "All right. Arizona is not a great place. It is the birthplace of the Desert Demons, there are a lot of sandstorms, and the red sky still has a presence there."

Red sky. That had been part of the aftermath of the Big Boom. As far as I knew, that meant radiated lighting strikes, and plenty of them.

"We don't gotta worry about the Demons, yeah?" Fisher asked.

Kyle shrugged. "Let's hope not. We'll be near the Grand Canyon, but the Demons usually keep to themselves. As for this mission, we are gonna storm a factory held by the NRF. We go in, capture a scientist, and interrogate them. The rest we terminate."

I rolled my eyes. "Whatever ends this war quicker."

We had four helicopters for this mission. This was gonna be a stealth mission for team A. They would sneak in, set the explosives around the factory, and detonate them. In the confusion we, Team B, would charge in to mop up the rest. I would head in with Fisher and Sera while Kyle led his own team to take over the factory for Miller Corps.

We touched down a few miles away from the factory. Arizona felt different from Nevada, for sure. There was a lot of sand, rock, and rubble. It was cloudy, and sand fell from the sky like rain. I climbed up to the roof of a destroyed general store and scouted with my cracked binoculars. "Not a lot of dudes there. This damn sand makes things harder, but I see enough. They're most likely squatting. Taking shelter, maybe."

Kyle was next to me, casually eating a sandwich. "Good. Things should go nice and smooth tomorrow."

I looked over and laughed. "Really? I never saw you this chill before."

"I learned from the best, dude."

He said dude very awkwardly.

"Please, no more. But that was dope, Kyle."

"Of course. Ready to end this, Dopeman?"

"You know it."

# CHAPTER TWENTY-FIVE
## HEAVEN CHASERS

Another day, another fight I'd have to win. I thanked God I had some friends to help me. I walked over to Kyle, who sat alone drinking water. I sat with him and smiled. He gave a smile back.

"You look tired," he said, looking out towards the sandy town. "You should sleep."

I shook my head. "Nah. Just tired of the war. How do you even do it?"

He chuckled. "I was thrust into war when I was a kid. I was only thirteen when the bombs dropped."

"You're young, eh? I couldn't tell. How did you survive at thirteen?"

"Yup. That's what they all ask. I was alone in my bunker. I think I was in summer school when the alarms went off. I went my own way and found this bunker that was open. I got in as the bombs fell. I was alone for months, it does something to a kid. It taught me to survive alone, it taught me that up here"—he pointed to his head—"is your greatest weapon."

I leaned back to soak up his story. "How did you join Miller Corps?"

"I joined at the start of the Intro Wars. I was in the middle of it, actually. I was getting shot at by all these bandit groups. It was Miller Corps that saved me. The general himself recruited me."

"Wow. I see. Crazy story. You came out to be a great man."

Kyle smiled and shook his head. "You too. All the stories you told me, it's about time I opened up myself."

"Well, about that... I was really curious about who I'm fighting for."

Kyle laughed. "You ask this now?"

"I was too busy getting shot at. Now tell me, soldier."

"Fine, fine. As far as I know, this guy named Vincent founded Miller Corporation in Russia in 2018. It was a rebel force meant to free the oppressed and defend them from the greedy generals that fight for the opposite of human rights. As they advanced, the corp got bigger, to the point where they thought to expand. Around 2063, they changed the army's name to just Miller Corps, and it became a full-on private army, an entire nation for hire. Then the Boom came around, stopping any plans from happening. Vance Miller was in charge once we resurfaced. The army was still mostly together. They'd been in Oakland on a mission and they saw the need for stability—a stability no one else could give us."

I nodded. "Damn."

"Yeah, damn. Enough about that, I'm telling a nicer story," Kyle said with a smile.

I laughed, sharing my joy with him.

It was mid-afternoon, the perfect time to strike. My team and I hiked over to the outskirts of the factory, using the sandstorm as cover. We had a red sky, and thunder rumbled in the background. Once we saw Team A go, we prepared to charge in. Fisher loaded his rifle, clearing his throat. "Don't take all the kills, yeah?"

I scoffed. "Don't be slow then, partner."

Sera shook her head. "You two watch how a real sharpshooter gets things done."

After a few quiet moments, the explosives went off. The blast shook the foundations of the factory, rocking the NRF soldiers. They got out, shaken and dazed as they yelled out to prepare the others for the fight. Team B charged in, ready to battle.

Fisher hung back, picking off three from afar. Sera clotheslined one and killed three with her massive revolver. She mercy killed the one she'd left gasping for air. I sliced and diced two, and blasted three with my shotgun. Fisher was able to keep us covered as we took out a chunk of the forces, but it wasn't sweet for long. One of the NRF men threw a pipe bomb, hitting ten of us, including me. The shrapnel punctured my hand and cheek. I was dazed, confused. I saw us quickly losing this fight. Our men dying, Sera and Fisher getting outnumbered. Something snapped. I pulled out the pieces of metal with no effort and charged, filled with this urge to kill. I sliced, dodged punches, and cut heads off. I then pulled out my SMG to shoot the men with deadly precision. I was at seventeen kills. I hopped off a wall, did a flip, and sprayed the remaining three hiding behind makeshift cover.

*Twenty.*

When I landed, I felt pain in my leg. I'd been shot. Before I could even try to fix it, I got slammed into the brick wall of the factory. I groaned, struggling to stand. I was shaking, trying to feel my arm again.

A large man with blond hair stepped over me, and he was angry. "I'll crush you, freak!" he yelled as he picked me up over his head, military press style, ready to break my back. I pulled my arm blade out to stab him in the spine. He yelled and dropped to his knees. I quickly got out of his grasp and aimed my shotgun at his face.

"You can't stop freedo—"

I pulled the trigger before he could finish, letting half his face free.

*Twenty-one.*

I walked back into the factory, watching the army clean-up the rest of the NRF. I went to find Kyle. I felt the pain of the bullet in my leg as I headed over to Kyle. "We found the scientist?" I asked. I turned and noticed the dead men in lab coats. They were sprawled across the floor, shot in the forehead or back. There was a blood-smeared door, closed.

Kyle pointed at the door, then walked over and knelt down in front of it. "This door is locked. For a reason, I hope." He pulled out a spare pipe bomb and stuck it to the door.

As I loaded non-lethal shots, Kyle aimed his gun at the bomb and shot, blowing the door to pieces. I charged into the smoke and saw an old-looking man. I shot him right in the chest. The blow knocked him to the floor—he was out.

"Got him!" I yelled.

"Good," Kyle said. "Let's head into phase two."

"Good," Kyle said. "Let's head into phase two."

# CHAPTER TWENTY-SIX
## WHEN THE RIGHTEOUS FIGHT BACK

I leaned on a wall, patching my leg up and calming down. I wasn't used to that feeling of blood lust, and it shook me.

Fisher walked up and helped me wrap my leg. "You alright?" he asked. "You looked like a different man out there."

I nodded slowly. "I'll be fine. Something just snapped in me. It felt like I could hunt anything down. It brought me joy to end these men's lives, Fisher. That wasn't me."

He sighed as he finished up my bandages. "Sounds like this war is affecting you more than you realize. You have to chill, Dopeman."

"I can't. I won't let Kyle down. I can't let you or Sera down. We have to end this war quickly."

"You know that's not gonna happen. They've been at it for quite a while. Who knows when the war is gonna stop?"

I stood, testing my leg. I could walk a little better now. "Maybe. I'll need to help get info from the scientist. Thanks, Fisher."

Fisher smiled and tapped my shoulder. "No problem, handsome. Stay safe."

Kyle used one of the factory rooms to interrogate the scientist. I walked in to find them both bloody, panting. Kyle punched him with his human hand, striking his eye socket. He had bruises all over his face and blood trickled from a cut on his forehead and the side of his mouth.

The scientist spit out blood. "Amerikanischer Hund!"

I walked up to Kyle. He sighed. "He's not talking. He's been speaking nothing but German for the past twenty minutes."

I shook my head. "Can he even speak English?"

"Yeah. He's just being difficult. Isn't that right, Becker?"

Becker laughed, then suddenly snapped his attention to me. "Dopeman?"

Guess I'd finally shed Foolish Courier. "Yeah, why? You're gonna finally speak my language?"

He frowned. "You've been the topic of all the NRF conversations after the Last Chance fight."

"You say this like you aren't a part of that group."

Becker shook his head, looking at me with his good eye. "No. They just enlisted my services."

"And what are these services?" I asked.

"I'll say... If that dog promises me freedom from whatever crimes their little group has me on."

I turned to Kyle. He rolled his eyes and nodded. "Deal. Now tell us what you know."

"I assume you speak of the Angel Waste. Angel Waste was a German creation. We had planned to drop it on the American populace. I was one of the lead scientists on the project." Becker smiled like he was proud of his actions. "The material is so unstable, so dynamic. It's almost like it's supernatural!"

"Whatever. What do you mean by dynamic? You can't get rid of it?"

"Not at all. It was made to assimilate with anything and everything designed to destroy it. If you try to burn it, the waste forms into the fire. And when you fools tried to blow it up it transformed into the bomb!"

I scratched my chin, taking in the information. "And then it mixed in the sky because of the rain and lighting."

"Correct! Such a perfect design!" He laughed like a mad man.

Kyle punched Becker with his metal arm, knocking him out. "He was annoying me."

"So, what now?" I asked.

"I have orders to follow before we head back to Nevada, but I'll let you rest, you need it."

"Thanks, Tann. I'll see you later."

I walked out of the factory and sat next to a wall on the far side of the entrance. I closed my eyes, listening to thunder crack around me, too tired to care about anything. I didn't know how much more my body could take. I felt the pain, the discomfort. I had to keep pushing. For my team.

Sera found me in my moment. She sat next to me silently. I lay my head on her shoulder. I didn't even say anything, and she could tell I was in pain. "No matter what, Dopeman. I will take care of you."

It was there I saw Dani again. She looked at me and tilted her head.

"Why are you looking at me?" she asked.

"Dani…" Tears welled up in my eyes. I shook my head.

"I need you to let me go. Say it to her. I know you want to say it."

I opened my eyes to look at Sera. "I like you, Sera."

She smiled and kissed me. "I like you too, Dopeman."

We then took a nap, in harmony.

That is, until a massive explosion snapped me awake. I was still confused; we'd slept so soundly we'd ignored the strong winds and the sudden thunder. I helped Sera up and ran to see NRF rushing up from the far end of the factory, shooting everyone. I wanted to find Fisher and Kyle, but Sera was too exposed. A guy had his gun trained on her. I dove in front of her. The bullet went through my side. It felt like hell was making a cameo in my body. I landed, pulled out my SMG, and killed him. All I could hear was the thunder and wind. I was too shocked to hear Sera screaming my name as she dragged me to safety. Through sheer will, I picked myself up and grit my teeth.

Sera looked terrified at my injuries. "Dopeman!"

"Let's—Gah! Let's go!" I leaned on Sera's arm and walked over to the factory exit away from the lost battle. By the time we headed outside, the sandstorm had gotten worse; I could hardly see in front of me. We barely saw the surviving group retreat. As we reached the others, the NRF noticed and shot at us. At the same time, lightning struck the middle of the group, sending usflying. I tumbled down a hill, hit my head, and was knocked out.

# CHAPTER TWENTY-SEVEN
## DOPEMAN, ALONE

Three weeks.

Three weeks I'd been alone and lost out in the Arizona wasteland. I was able to crawl my way over into a cave, mending my wounds with a Miller Corps emergency first aid kit. It was hell for the first few days, as the wound gel mended my side and I contended with a splitting headache. But the gel worked fast and after a day, I was able to get back on my feet to survey the landscape. While I was able to sip on my canteen and survive off rations, the sandstorms and red sky made it basically impossible to see any landmark, so I decided to stick to my cave till I knew where to go. As I sat at the campfire, watching the wood burn, hearing the wind howl and thunder boom in the distance, I felt off. This was the first time in the last several months that I didn't have anyone. I was usually a lone wolf anyways. Ever since I'd first donned the straw bucket hat and gray gear, I'd been alone. I rested my head on the cold, hard surface. I closed my eyes, and dreamed about those days.

* * *

Those days. I say it like they were good.

They were just as bad as now, actually.

As I saw Dani bleed out, a wave of great anger shot over me. I had to retaliate. I hadn't killed in years, but I had to at this moment. I made a grave for both Dani and the old man, and over the next month I trained by myself. I learned how to use the shotgun properly, and I kept tinkering with explosives. Eventually I figured out how to modify certain shells. I was able to really spice up the powder with a hint of radiation to get high-explosive shells. I could only make two with the materials I had, but I knew how to make more. I also took the old man's gear, something he'd worn to war in the Middle East. It was light, offered good protection, and it looked good on me. Finally, I got his bucket hat to complete the look. While training I also snuck around the destroyed buildings and saw a lot of fighting on the streets. The Intro War was in full swing, and I wanted nothing to do with it. I tracked a few guys who wore exactly what Dani's killers had worn, and finally, I got a location. They camped right above the golden gate bridge. I was finally ready to get revenge. One night I snuck out, fully prepared to have the fight of my life.

I climbed down to hang under the bridge and got a full view of the camp. Fifteen men living an uneasy alliance. That was the norm at the start of the wars. Small groups not trusting anyone. Eventually, I got down and used a rock as cover, loading both of my explosive shells. I aimed and fired, sending most of the camp up in flames. I got rid of nine guys with two hits. Then I ran into mop up with my pistol. I shot at two before two more tackled me. I was able to blast one in the chest before the other knocked my shotgun away. He punched me in the jaw and nose before I found a rock to bash his head in. I got on top, placed a knee on his chest, and finished the job. I then got hit in the head with a rock. I fell forward face first, playing dead. My head was bleeding, so he didn't finish the job.

I scrambled over to my shotgun and loaded my shells; I shot his top off before he even noticed I was alive. My head was badly damaged, but I had to deal with one more. He was injured. Half his body was charred by the explosion. He was gargling blood. I smirked and left him to die. I limped home, collapsing as I was tending to my head.

I didn't wanna step foot in San Fran anymore. After fully recovering, I headed east for a new life as...

I didn't know. Not yet, anyways. I tried to run from the name, but I couldn't run from the debt. The debt of Dopeman.

# CHAPTER TWENTY-EIGHT
## ÇALL ME IF YOU GET LOST [ÖR ÇAPTURED]

Another week passed before the weather finally cleared up. As I waited, I gathered water from condensation during the night; it was barely enough to keep me going. Other than that, I thought of the past. I hated my act of violence. It was unnecessary. I'd already killed the ones who killed Dani. I'd had that bloodlust, similar to what I'd felt in the factory. I tried to keep myself light-hearted, but it gets hard when your back is against the wall.

When I finally spotted blue sky, I stepped out into the sunlight, seeing the Arizona wasteland clearly for the very first time. Compared to Nevada, there was a lot more stone and grass than sand, but this was a desert. I started to walk, using my gut feeling to pick a direction, hoping it would take me to some sort of civilization. I wasn't hopeful I'd find anything, but I had to try. Hours passed, and I started to doubt I was getting anywhere. I looked at the sky. Was the sun even moving? Where the hell was I? I started to feel the first signs of fatigue, losing feeling in my legs and falling down a grassy dune. I shook the dirt and sand off and downed the last of my water. This was it, wasn't it? I accepted my fate and collapsed next to a rock as the sun went down, accepting what was to come.

Ahh, finally. The sweet release. I could feel it coming. Death used to be scary. But now, with all the stress and pain fading with my life, I was relieved.

**"Hey!"** I heard.

I opened my eyes to see Sera. I tilted my head in confusion.

**"Who told you to die? Not me!"**

"Sera…I'm so tired. I can't go on."

**"Yes, you can. Dopeman, You're stronger than that. I know this."**

"Sera…"

**"Wake up!"**

I snapped awake to gunshots. After stumbling to my feet, I ran over a hill to see a group of NRF soldiers executing Miller Corps soldiers. This was bad. I loaded my shotgun and surveyed the area. There looked to be three NRF soldiers. Normally they'd be easy targets, but I was dehydrated and limping. As long as the Miller Corps men had time to run, I could distract those NRF dudes, then go in for the kill.

With a quick breath, I yelled, "Hey! Dopeman here!"

I fired at one of the men, hitting him in the shoulder. The force of it knocked him over, but failed to pierce his armor. He got up unharmed. As the NRF started toward me, the Miller Corps men ran as fast as they could. I wasted my last four shots on the other two men with no success. Then I turned to run.

Too slow. They came up the hill, flanking me on either side. As one soldier attempted to punch me, I dodged and stabbed him in the neck with my arm blade. He fell, but I wasn't quick enough to avoid a kick to the chest. I fell down the hill, coughing. He kicked me again to keep me down and aimed his gun at me. With an evil grin on his face, he whacked me over the head, knocking me out.

# CHAPTER TWENTY-NINE
## GODHAND: LEADER OF FREEDOM

I was getting tired of blows to the head.

My hands were bound and I was too tired to try to free myself. I sat in a haze and only fully gained consciousness once somebody threw water on my face. I coughed violently, licking whatever water was left on my cracked lips.

I looked around. I was in a small room with cracked concrete walls. I saw a table and three people. From the way they all flocked and answered to the one in the middle, he was the one I had to contend with. He had long black dreadlocks and wore a worn-out denim jacket. It had the massive NRF shield logo, patches of the Jamaican flag, and flags of bygone mercenary groups from the Intro Wars. He turned, showing off his dark skin, scarred face, and brown eyes. "Dopeman," he said. His thick, Jamaican accent hummed in my ears.

I wanted to say something, but my throat was so dry that all I could do was cough.

The Jamaican looked at one of the guards. "Bring di mon sum wata now."

The guard complied, and tilted half a glass of water against my lips.

"You might be wondering why ya still yer life right now," he said. I shrugged in response. "I've heard from the road you're just some Ragamuffin with a bounty on his head. You don't even believe what fightin' for, do ya Dopeman?" He must've spoken in Jamaican Patois, but tried to speak proper English so I could understand.

"I... I Just wanna be a courier again."

"Then join me, Dopeman. You n' me."

I shook my head. "I don't even know who you people are."

"The NRF wants the freedom we longed for even before we mashed up the world. Your government ruined my life. I was in Kingston with my lady and two pickney dem. My life was flawless until Hurricane Genesis. My wife was dead. Me n' the children had nowhere to go. Then some white people with their charity come round. They offered me n' the kids a chance to come to Merika. This place... bad like the rest of the world. They always say pull yuhself up by unnu bootstraps, but there was nothing to hold on to. Everywhere I go, I would be denied, told to go home. Soon I had no home to come round to. My kids were tek aweh. I was alone, had nobody thanks to yer systems and culcha." He approached me and poked my chest. He spoke with bitterness. "I was ova in Cali when the Big Boom happened. That was the greatest day to happen to Merika. It was a chance to staat ova. I walked out of the bunker to fighting. People dyin'. I made these people unite under one flag, Dopeman. The flag of freedom." He smiled, his arms outstretched. "Di people called me Godhand. I was a prophet of freedom. Then I see Miller Corps come round, trying to bring the same system that ruined my life. I have to get rid of them, ya know?"

I shook my head. "I'm sorry, but anarchy will only lead to chaos sooner or later."

"You're blind. You'll see once we wipe off di Miller Corps." Godhand turns to the guards. "Put him inna prison. I'm gwine tan deh fah while." They nodded and picked up my weakened body, dragging me out of the room. My vision was blurring, so I couldn't see much.

They put me down in some old-world prison, barely holding on to functionality. The busted walls gave me a view of the hall outside, the yelling and ranting of prisoners and the casual conversation of guards as they walked past. I was thrown into a cell. As I hit the cold concrete, I passed out.

And here I thought I'd escaped jail time.

# CHAPTER THIRTY
## PRISONERS OF WAR

Man...

I felt warm. Like I was in somebody's arms. I was offered water. I drank happily.

Was all that some bad dream? Was I back at camp?

Nope.

I opened my eyes to see a massive man giving me water through a bowl. "You're awake!" he said in a deep voice. He had bronze-colored skin and long, disheveled gray hair that matched his unkempt beard. He had deep wrinkles on his forehead and cheeks, showing his age. "There, there. You'll be okay."

A woman behind the old dude was also staring. She was a frowning redhead. She had her hair in a ponytail and taped-up glasses on her face. She sported a deep cut on her cheek. She paced around the cell, clearly worried. "He's not five, Carter. He could be some killer or..."

Carter continued to rock me slowly. "He's just some poor soul. Look at him. He couldn't hurt a fly. Right, stranger?"

I finished drinking and looked back at him. "Why am I in your arms?"

He shrugged. "Genny says it's more comfortable than the beds they give us—"

"Stop!" Genny yelled. Embarrassed, she sat.

Carter laughed as I moved to get up on my own. To be fair, it was comfortable, and I felt a little better after that water. But I was hungry, too. I saw some stale bread on a plate, so I picked it up to take a bite. I looked down at my attire. It was a gray jumpsuit marked with certain numbers on the pants , probably used to identify us if our bodies rotted thanks to the beautiful conditions of the prison. I was 1717, Carter was 2002, and Genny was 7025. I sat and ate.

Carter and Genny were bickering. Carter relaxed on the floor as Genny got back up to pace around the small space we shared. "Come on, Gen. Lighten up. There's dinner in a few hours. It's grass and Demon eggs night, my favorite!"

Genny wasn't amused. "It's ALWAYS grass and eggs."

"And it's wonderful! What would you rather have?

"A bullet to the brain."

Carter wagged his index finger. "Not very healthy."

Genny rolled her eyes and turned to me. "And who are you, stranger?" She had a Spanish accent.

"I go by Dopeman. Nice to meet you... Genny, is it?"

She chuckled. "Dopeman? That's kind of a stupid name."

Carter kicked her playfully. "Gen, that's rude."

She shrugged. "What? It's not a real name."

I finished the bread and laughed. "It's cool, It's cool. I just can't remember my real name."

"Then why don't you make a new one?" Carter asked.

I looked down at the damaged floor, not knowing the answer. "Maybe when I retire from my job."

Genny looked surprised. "You work? Is there a civilization out there?"

"Yeah. I work as a courier. How long have you two been here?"

They both frowned. Eventually, Carter said, "Nine years. The rest of the prisoners have been in here for about seven or six."

"You've been here since what, the Intro Wars?"

They both nodded.

I felt bad. "Geez…"

Carter patted me on the back. "It's quite alright. We've kind of accepted this, ya know?"

"Aw come on, you haven't thought of escaping?"

Genny rolled her eyes. "Of course, we have. But we don't know where to go. Hell, we didn't even know that there were still towns. We just stuck to what was safe."

As I started to reply, Godhand walked up to the cell door. He kneeled, laughing. "Deh a nuh civilization. Only war. Death. And I have di power to stop it. How does it feel, Dopeman? How does it feel stopping di path ah freedom?"

"Piss off," I snapped.

"Uh-huh." Godhand stood up, smirking. "Hab fun a si yuh fren dem parish, Dopeman." He walked away. I stood up and leaned on the bars, glaring after him.

"We're getting out of here," I mumbled.

Carter and Genny looked at me, confused.

"I promise, you'll see freedom when I'm done here."

# CHAPTER THIRTY-ONE

## HAPPY BODY, SAD PAST

Over the next month, I prepared my body for the future breakout around the prison schedule. We woke up each morning at about 6 A.M, ate breakfast, worked on repairing the prison, had freetime, lunch, more freetime, dinner, and sleep. I asked Carter and Genny to work out. We would spend one month getting our bodies to peak condition, and another month looking for any weaknesses in the camp. This month was workout time. Genny hated physical activity, so she did extra scouting. I was usually alone with the big man, working intensely to get my failing body back in shape. I usually worked out shirtless, so Carter saw my scarred and bandaged body. One day, we finished the first half of our pull-ups, using a metal bar we stuck in the wall. I hopped down after reaching fifty.

"Good job, son!" Carter yelled, hopping up to do his own fifty.

I smirked and leaned back, watching him go. "Thanks, dude. So, how old are ya?"

He grunted and looked at me. "Fifty-five. How about you?"

"Twenty-nine. So, you've known Genny for long?"

"Yeah. From a little while before the bombs dropped. I took care of her."

"Really? What happened to her?"

He reached thirty. "Not my story to tell. You work alone, Dopeman?"

"I used to. Then I got myself tangled in a war."

"The war is still going on?" he asked, reaching forty.

"Not the same one. You know about Miller Corps?"

"Yeah. Back then they were just a merc group like everybody else. So NRF and Miller Corps are the only groups left?"

"On the west coast, yeah."

Carter stepped down and moved back. "Goodness. It's been so long."

I got back on the pole to work. "That's why we're getting out. All of us."

A week went by, and I felt great. I was starting to feel happy again.

Carter and I were in the field lifting weights a few days later while watching Genny scream at the other prisoners in Spanish while playing cards. This was one of the first times I'd started to build muscle mass. "So," Carter said suddenly. "You look like you've been through a lot."

I laughed. "That's what war does. You were in the Intro Wars; you know a thing or two, don't you?"

"Yeah, but I don't think I want to push myself that bad."

"Sometimes you had to, yeah? Push yourself beyond your limits. It's the only way of getting things done."

"No, no, son. Think of it like this: You're driving a car. If the car breaks down, you're gonna stop and make sure the car is okay before you continue, right?"

I nod, extending my arms for another rep.

"If you keep pushing the car, the car eventually is going to stop working. You understand?"

"Yeah. I get it. It's so hard to not push. I think I'm gonna let my friends down."

"If your friends are strong enough to survive in a war this long, I think they can handle themselves."

I put the weights back and flexed. "You're pretty dope, old man."

He laughed and hugged me. "That's my boy!"

"Relax! Relax! You're still sweaty!"

Another two weeks went by, and I was feeling like my old self again. Ironically, this was the best thing to happen to me in some time.

In the last week of January, we focused on striking and combat training. I was hitting a restored punching bag while Carter held it. I wanted to know a bit more about the man. "So how did you end up here?"

He hummed. "Surprised it took you this long to ask that question."

"Well, I didn't want to ask personal questions like that. I didn't want to remind you of anything."

"Listen, Dopeman. You told me all these stories about you and your life, I think it's fair for you to know." I softened my strikes so he could concentrate. "We were in Phoenix when the bombs dropped. We found this large bunker with a small community. It turned out to belong to this militia leader. We all opened the bunker, armed. That was Gen's first time holding a gun. We called ourselves Riley's Naturals or just RN. We must've looked threatening, 'cause some other group shot at us. We defended our people. The next thing we know, we had all kinds of groups attack us. It was a bloody mess. Which sucks for me because I tried to be a pacifist."

"Hard to do so in this world."

"I know..." Carter sighed as I finished. We sat against a wall, looking through the cell bars. "I didn't want to be this strong. But anyways, we fought for about a year straight, then some big guys with advanced gear started to mop up the other groups. We couldn't prepare fast enough. Next thing you know, half my friends are gone. Some dread-haired guy preaches to me about freedom and joining his cause when I'm captured. The prick had his guys beat me half to death so of course, I said no. And what he tried to do to Genny..."

I leaned forward. "You're not a fan of Godhand, huh?"

"I'll crush his head when I get the chance."

"Great!" I clapped happily. "Let's get you closer to that goal, yeah?"

# CHAPTER THIRTY-TWO

## MI AMOR

As February rolled around, my four-week training camp did numbers for my body. I'd become lean and ripped. Genny was working out a little as well, and it showed. We walked the yard, scoping it out.

Genny pointed to the wall. "We're surrounded by badly aged walls. All I know is that they're too thick to carve through and too tall to climb over without getting sniped down."

I scanned the area. At the top of the wall I saw sharpshooters, pacing back and forth. They wore light armor on the chest, with tan shorts and boots to combat the desert hybrid heat. It narrowed our escape options considerably. "Badly aged? These walls look clean to me."

"On the surface..." She knocked on one specific part of the wall. "They restored this place, true. But about five years ago, the wall collapsed. They fixed it up, but not well enough."

I walked up to the wall, knocking and feeling on it. "Hmm. We need something huge. It'll take months for us to carve it with a spoon or something. We need something immediate."

"Like?"

"Let me sit on it. I need to think." I leaned on the wall, looking at the cloudy sky. Another sandstorm would arrive soon. Gen stayed with me, so I decided to conversate. "What ya do for fun?"

She leaned toward me, thinking. "Chess or cards. I love to play poker."

"Oh? When did you get that hobby?"

"Mexicali. I would play with my father when I was done with work. He was a pro, let me tell ya."

"Where did you work?"

"Tattoo artist. I did some tats here. Half these boys are tatted up because of me."

I laughed. "Oh yeah? Where's yours?"

"It's covered by my jumpsuit. Maybe later you can see it." She winked and laughed. I chuckled back. "So, you're a mail boy? What made you want to deliver packages everywhere?"

"Hmm... Maybe it's because I never felt comfortable sitting down. I went to the east coast, but I loved to adventure, see what changed in this world. It just so happened everyone called me Foolish Courier." I smiled.

"You're a funny guy, that's for sure."

After a week, I figured it out: A pipe bomb!

"A pipe bomb?" Gen said in disbelief. We were in the lunchroom. She was smoking and kicking my ass at chess. "And how would we even make it?"

"I'm good with my hands. All I need is a piece of metal, a few live wires, and gunpowder. Preferably shotgun shells."

She sighed and thought it over. "Fine. I'll find some way to get the shells. In the meantime, I got some news."

"Shoot, Bosslady."

"I got some connections that sneak around. You know some bootlickers clean up the guard areas? It just so happens I tattoo them, and they pay me back with info. I got two things from them this morning."

"Show em."

Genny pulled out a blueprint. It looked like a metal rig made to be worn over the body. The rig had panels made to enhance the user's reflexes. "This is the exo suit. You know about AKMs?"

I nodded. I'd heard of Automated Killing Machines from before the war. "Those Japanese cyborgs? Yeah, why?"

"Androids. But back in the day, Americans wanted to counter the unstoppable androids by making humans as powerful as them. They also got blueprints of some kind of... laser sword? No, it's plasma." She looked confused as she pulled out another blueprint.

I shook my head. "I fully doubt that they have built an exo suit and a whole sword made of plasma. Now what's the other thing?"

"Let's see..." She pulled out a small tape player and pressed play.

I heard walking, and the sound of a chant.

"Di Miller Corps a causing chubble near di Grand Canyon. Mi wi bi gaan mid April tuh git rid ah dem. Desert Demons fi mi also bi ah problem Suh keep yuh guard up. Wi fight fah freedom. Wi a di leaders ah ah out a road wurl. Dismissed."


End of recording.


"Mid-April? He's leaving in mid-April?" I asked.

"Yup. That gives us plenty of time to prepare. Checkmate, estúpido."

"Crap."

It was near the end of February. I was tinkering with the frame of the pipe bomb. Carter was asleep and Genny sat next to me as I perfected the shape. "How did you meet Carter?"

Gen rested her head on her hands. "I moved to Arizona with my girlfriend. I was young and dumb. I would have followed that girl anywhere. She was good at twisting words, manipulating me, gaslighting me. She even turned me against my dad. My own padre. She convinced me to move away. By the time I realized she was hurting me, it was too late. It was a trap. She controlled my life. I had no money to head back home so I ran away. It was there that I met Carter, when I was on the brink. So hungry, starving."

I nodded. "You're a strong woman, Genny. I'm proud."

"So are you, Dopeman. Now get to work, loser." She pushed my head playfully.

*What a woman.*

# CHAPTER THIRTY-THREE

## Before The Tournament

I'd gotten much better at combat by the time March arrived, and no longer had to use underhanded tactics to get things done. I was doing soft sparring with Carter one day, practicing a few advanced moves. I did a double kick to finish off the training. "Great job, son!" he yelled. I laughed and shook hands with him. In a week the guards would run a fighting tournament to relieve some stress from the war. The winner would get a nice clock and some food. Sure, it sounded useless now, but I needed that clock because it was an old-world clock. Those things had a tiny amount of radioactive components and high volatile wires. Perfect for a pipe bomb. These clowns were big, strong. They weren't quick like me though.

After my training, I sat with my trainer, scouting my competition. The sixteen-man bracket had been released about an hour ago, and I wanted to see who was my first round competition. Carter pointed to a smaller man. He had a messy afro and stubble. "They call him The Ant," Carter started. "Ant is the small, tough dude type. He's going to be quicker than you, so you'll have to overpower the man, got it?"

I nodded and looked around. "Anybody else of note?"

"Eh…" Carter smacked his lips. "On the other side of the bracket, there's a woman who's undefeated. They call her Kaos." He pointed to a dangerous-looking woman sitting surrounded by underlings. She was Asian, covered in tattoos, and she had short black hair with slight streaks of gray. Flowers and dragons traveled across her body. "Rumor has it she was a Yakuza. She moved to Arizona to retire early. Once the bombs dropped, she thought she could win the Intro Wars, so she resisted the NRF with her own army. Of course she lost. As punishment, she was dealt the shame of capture."

"Why does she even fight?"

Carter gives me a shrug. "Nobody knows. She just beats everyone silently and takes the food."

"Thankfully, I got myself on the opposite side of the bracket."

We walked back to the cell room once yard time was over. "So, what were you like before the bombs dropped?" I asked.

"Herbalist. I love plants."

"Oh? You like working out on the side too, yeah?"

"Well, I come from a long line of wrestlers. My dad was one of the best, actually. I didn't like to hurt people, though. I liked nature. He didn't care, so he made me become big and strong. I can't complain, but I'd rather have the choice."

I shook my head slowly. "I know a guy who'd love you."

"Oh? He must like wrestling."

"I wouldn't be surprised..."

A few nights before the tournament, Gen tapped me awake. "You got no ink. I need to change that."

"What?" I groaned, sitting up.

"You're in prison now, it should be a rule at this point."

"I have given zero thought to a tattoo." I slowly took off my shirt. I might as well. Who was I to say no to anything free?

Genny got her makeshift needles and ink. "I got an idea," she said proudly.

I lay on the bed, and she got to work on my back. After about an hour she started on my shoulders. Then I sat up to have her work on my chest as well. Eventually, she finished. I stood and turned, using a piece of broken glass as a mirror. Seven faces, all with different expressions, circled my back. I smiled. I liked the design. "And who are they?" I asked.

"The seven gods of luck. Japanese thing. I thought it was pretty cool, considering all the stories you told."

"Yeah, it's dope! My chest..." I turned to see that my right pec had a tarot card on it. Of course, it was the fool. "Clever," I said, laughing.

"You know me. Ready to kick ass, Dopeman?"

"Of course!"

# CHAPTER THIRTY-FOUR

## The Tournament Of Dogs, Part One

The time had come. There was no formal name for the tournament, but the prisoners coined it "The Tournament of Dogs." We all gathered around the yard, forming a makeshift ring for the contestants to fight in.

The first round was Kaos against Skye. Skye was some tough guy from Riley's Naturals. He was of average build, with the tattoos of a former gang member. It would be a great chance to see Kaos in action. The warden stepped to the middle and spoke.

"Listen up! Welcome to the tournament. You all know the rules. No killing. No running. Other than that, it's fair game. Now, I want Skye and Kaos up here first. Let's get this show on the road." The crowd cheered as the pair got ready to fight.

Genny and Carter were talking behind me.

"I got a pack of smokes that Kaos snaps his hand," Carter chimed.

"I got two saying she'll go for the arm," Genny replied.

I scoffed as the fight started. Skye was in a boxing pose and Kaos was in a kickboxing stance. Skye tested the waters, throwing quick jabs and backing up; Kaos dodged them effortlessly. Perhaps he was getting too comfortable, because he didn't see the quick kick to his side coming. It was sudden, and by the sound of the impact it hit like a brick. Kaos took advantage of Skye's recoil and took a hold of his head. She proceeded to put her knees to his face, destroying it with her knee lifts. Eventually, Skye pushed her away, drunkenly trying a right hook. Kaos caught it, kicked his legs out to bring him to his knees, and drove her knee into his arm, snapping it in half. He screamed, but was quickly silenced by a final kick to the jaw. He lay on the ground, shaking. She silently stood over him for a moment, then walked away. The crowd went wild.

"Pay up, old man!" Gen yelled.

Carter groaned. "Shoot!"

That was a dangerous woman.

The warden summoned people to drag Skye away. "Next up, I want Dopeman and Mobly."

"It's The Ant!" The small man chimed, stepping out. I did the same, removing my top.

"Good luck, man," I said, smiling.

He laughed. "Yeah, for you!"

The fight started. The Ant showed his speed early, going for a quick jab. I spun out of the way and tripped him, backing up. He'd hoped to hit me again, but I moved so effortlessly. I felt amazing. I stopped on a dime and went for one big punch in the gut, then a mighty kick to the head. His head bounced off the unforgiving dirt. I backed up as Ant stumbled to his feet. He flipped me off. I laughed as I ran in for a massive dropkick to the face, landing on my feet as he crashed to the floor, knocked out. I smiled and shrugged before moving on.

Dopeman was back.

# CHAPTER THIRTY-FIVE

## THE TOURNAMENT OF DOGS, PART TWO

I headed back to the crowd to watch the rest of the fights. I love a good, old-fashioned fistfight.

The Outlaw got destroyed by Mugen. Jade put Speed to the ground with his submission holds and moved to the next round. Rose took Avon down with relative ease. Surd barely defeated Wage to punch his ticket to face Kaos in the next round. Fuji whacked Don. Finally, Monsoon washed Xavier to face Bozo in the next round.

As I got ready to join in, the Ant stepped in front of me.

I put my hands on my hips. "Hey, short stack. Could you step out of my way?"

The Ant laughed and stumbled, still feeling the effects of the fight. "You think you'll beat Okuda? Ha! You're nothing compared to him!"

I rolled my eyes and looked at the warden in the middle of the ring, getting ready to announce the next fight.

"Yo!" the warden yelled. "We're in the semi-conference finals now. I want Dopeman and Okuda up next."

I walked out and my opponent did the same. He knelt and prayed before standing. He had a man bun and a clean-shaven face.

"I must defeat you," he said, taking a Tae Kwon Do stance. The fight started.

Okuda went in for heavy-handed strikes, almost breaking through my blocks with each blow. He finally caught me with a hit to the jaw. I hopped back as he went for a mean left hook. I rolled under it and he punched the ground, missing me. He shook his hand and gritted his teeth  as we reset. I went on the offensive, breaking down his defense with punches and kicks. He dodged, and I dodged his strikes as well. I finally found an opening, driving my fist in his face. He moved back, and I capitalized on my advantage with another few hits to the face. He dodged the last one, going for one last hit. I caught it, hearing a loud smack as it hit my hand. I judo flipped Okuda, driving my knee into his spine. He hit the ground, rolling and holding his back. I ran over and placed my knee on his neck, my fist in the air.

"Hey! Tap out!" I yelled.

After struggling with a bloody nose, he tapped, meaning I would move on. I stood and put my hands up, then moved to find Genny to put me on ice.

The warden clapped his hands and let the crowd go wild. "Kaos. Surd. You're up."

They stepped into the bloody circle. Surd instantly ran towards Kaos, going for a flying kick. Kaos caught his foot and swung him over her head, slamming him to the ground. She ruthlessly kicked his ribs, back, and legs. Eventually, Surd kicked away, scrambling to stand. It was too late. Kaos was quick, driving a foot into his face. She stomped on his face a few more times, staining the dirt with his blood. She put her feet on his chest. He tapped with his free hand.

"Koshinuke…" she said.

The crowd went silent. This was most likely the first time she'd spoken in a while.

Gen shook her head. "Everyone knows—"

"Not to tap out when you fight Kaos," Carter finished.

She repeatedly stomped on his face, screaming. "Koshinuke! Koshinuke!! Koshinuke!!! KOSHINUKE!!!"

Nobody came to stop her, but he was alive…

Barely.

# CHAPTER THIRTY-SIX

## THE TOURNAMENT OF DOGS, PART THREE

They dragged the poor soul's body away. It was time for the other fighters to go. Fiji beat Bozo in a bloody contest, ending with Bozo's leg being snapped in half. Jadesaw was able to make Rose tap out, meaning he joined me in the next round.

The warden proudly stepped up. "Conference finals! Kaos, Fuji. Step up."

They both got ready. Fuji bowed; Kaos stared blankly at him. They charged simultaneously, keeping the same intensity with each other. The fight had little to no defense whatsoever. They took turns kicking, punching, and slamming each other. Fuji chopped her neck and kicked her square in the chest. Kaos put both her knees in his gut, then face, keeping a tight grip on his head with those ruthless blows. Kaos saw an opening after Fuji dodged for the first time in the fight. He moved, dragging his left leg a little too much. Kaos jumped, then drove her legs down on Fuji's leg, bending it in the wrong place. She followed up with a blow to the head. The fight was over, but Kaos was brutal with a final punt kick to the head. She moved on to the finals.

The Ant and Okuda were behind me, looking on as the crowd cheered the woman's name.

"You think you can beat that?" Okuda asked me.

I looked back. "Yup!"

The group laughed as Warden called up the remaining fighters. "Randal. Dopeman."

"I really wish you'd call me Jadesaw, Warden…" he said as he stepped up.

He looked only too happy to fight me. It was weird.

He was a nimble man for sure. He hopped on me and took me down with a hurricanrana. I landed on my back, so he took advantage of that by putting me in an armbar. I grunted as he stretched my arm, trying to break it. I powered out by standing and using my free hand to repeatedly punch him in the face. He let go. I stamped him in the face, but he caught my foot before I could take it back. He pulled me to the ground, trying to break my leg. Not today. I kicked the fool right in the groin, and again in the face. I got to my hands and knees and finished him with two swift strikes to the face. I hyped the crowd with my victory, but my joy turned to dread as I looked at Kaos. Her cold, dead eyes stared at me.

How was I gonna beat her?

# CHAPTER THIRTY-SEVEN

## THE TOURNAMENT OF DOGS, PART FOUR

Only Kaos and I remained. I didn't know if I'd win, so I needed a backup plan. We got a three minute break before the finals. I walked up to Kaos, only to be met by her lackeys. Before they could do anything, Kaos waved her hand, beckoning.

I sat next to her. "Hey, Kaos…"

"No," she said. She seemed to know what I was planning.

"I need that clock. I'm gonna bust us all out of here. All I need is that clock and you'll be free."

She looked at me. "Earn your freedom."

"You don't want to leave?"

"You honestly think you can get out?"

I nodded.

The warden called for us. Kaos sighed and stood. "I'm sorry." She walked off.

Damn, it looked like I would be doing this the hard way.

I walked into the circle, getting prepared. I had to clear my mind from the rabid crowd and focus on Kaos.

The warden stood between us to make an announcement. "We have reached the finals! You all know who this woman is. The former Yakuza, hailing from Japan, KAAAAOSSSS!"

Kaos stood still, staring at me. "This guy is a newcomer. The definite rookie of the year, from parts unknown, DOPEMAAAAN!" I flexed to the crowd.

Warden signaled for the fight to start. Kaos kept a calm stance, and I did as well. At the same time, we hit each other in the jaw and we both stepped back. I immediately attempted a kick, but she caught it. She tried to go for a swipe at my other leg like Skye, but I used that leg to kick her right in the head. She let go, and I thudded to the ground. Kaos came after me like she hadn't felt a thing. I was getting up when she grabbed my head for those infamous knee lifts. She gave me four of them right to the head, breaking my nose. Blood spewed everywhere. As she went for a fifth. I caught it, pushing it down. I double punched her in the gut, broke free of her grip, and punched her right in the nose, breaking it for the first time in this tournament. I had no time to think about my busted nose or bleeding lip, I had to charge. I continued the fight, punching her with hard lefts and rights. A final uppercut sent her flying, but she landed on her feet. I didn't expect that, so I wasn't prepared for her to charge me and deal me a set of punches. She added a few kicks that almost shattered my ribs. A hard roundhouse kick sent me to the ground, coughing blood. That was a good one, I could almost feel myself going out. I stood, but she punched me again. And again. And again. I was on my back looking at the sky.

I was dazed, confused.

Once again, I was hurt. I was gonna lose.

It was then that I saw them.

Sera. Fisher. Kyle. Harper. Serena. Carter. Genny. All of my friends told me the same thing.

**"Get up, Dopeman!"**

I stumbled to my feet, blood all over my face. The crowd went wild. I slowly shook my head. She was looking at me angrily. We both yelled. I punched her, she lost some blood, she punched me, I lost some more. I gained an advantage when she lost her balance. I kept hammering her with my right hook. She was getting wobbly. She caught my hand and pulled us both to the ground. We scrambled to get on top, taking turns striking each other in the face. She won the struggle, hitting again and again. In a final act of desperation, I started homing in on her gut. She winced in pain, giving me a chance to get on top. I slipped, however, landing at her side. I hadn't given up yet. I latched on to her back, wrapping my arms around her neck. I squeezed, refusing to let go. She was driving her elbow at my ribs repeatedly, making me cough up blood. I kept my hold. In fact, I tightened it. I was fading, the hits were finally getting to me. I couldn't do it, so I let go, passing out.

When I awoke, Kaos was standing. She was holding on by a thread. Once Warden declared her the winner, she finally fell to the ground, collapsing next to me. She stared at me, panting.

I raise my eyebrows. "Wha...?"

"Anata wa umaku yatta, Dopeman."

I didn't know what that meant, but I nodded.

"You can have the clock..." Kaos passed out.

I looked to the sky and closed my eyes.

# CHAPTER THIRTY-EIGHT

## FREEDOM RINGS

A few weeks went by.

Kaos and I became decent friends. In the heat of the fight, we'd forged a bond that couldn't be broken. Once Gen had smuggled the shotgun shell I needed, I was able to construct the bomb with the broken fragments of the clock. After hours of frustrating wirework and getting the powder in, the bomb was finally ready. Our key to freedom.

Carter stared at the bomb. "So, what's the plan? We can't just plant the bomb and run, can we?"

I shook my head. "I have a plan, but I'll need Kaos to help us out."

I summoned Kaos to our cell. She sat quietly and looked at me.

Gen looked over. "Um, hi."

Kaos waved slightly. Carter laughed.

"Okay, here's the plan." I kneeled, drawing a rough image of the prison with a shiv. "I want Carter and Gen on the ground. I want 'em spreading the good news, make sure we get those boys riled up. Meanwhile, I'll be with Kaos sneaking into the prison to open the jail doors and get all the gear the NRF confiscated from us. When those doors are open, you two run in the yard and bomb that wall, we'll give you your gear, and then we run. Any questions?"

They all shook their heads. Kaos stood and left, and we all headed to bed early.

The next afternoon, we were all in the yard, looking at how the guards moved. Of course, we had a red sky. Godhand and a good chunk of his force were gone. With my shiv in hand, we ran into the restricted area. I stabbed four men on patrol by sneaking around and forcing my shiv into their necks. Kaos broke necks and choked out three more.

We finally reached the storeroom. I looked for Carter's old armor and Gen's rifle. Kaos put on her gear, which consisted of body armor and loose combat pants. I also put my stuff back on. A little tight around the arms, but it fit well enough.

When I put my sand cape on, Kaos looked at it. "It's blank."

I nodded. "Yeah, that a problem?"

"Give it." She cracked open a can of white paint that had been used to paint the walls and proceeded to paint Japanese characters on my cape. "Dopeman," she said, answering the question in my head.

"Thanks. Now, let's get to work."

# CHAPTER THIRTY-NINE

## THE BREAKOUT

With two more guards dead, it was time to press the button to release the prisoners.

"Let's go!" I yelled, letting the cell doors release. Before I left, I looked at a map pinned to the wall in the control room. Now I knew where I should go. I could hear the commotion already, with two guards armed and charging at us. Time to show them what I was made of. I dodged a baton attack and released my arm blade. I stabbed the guard right in the back. I felt amazing. I was really back. Kaos strong-armed the other and popped him in the face with a personalized pistol. I ran outside with her, to where the prisoners were fighting each other and setting fires. Lightning and thunder struck as the sky turned crimson. I looked around. The bomb should've gone off by no—

*BOOM!*

Never mind. Once I saw Carter and Genny, I passed them their gear and they quickly equipped it, watching the chaos unfold. The prisoners scrambled to leave, though the guards kept the effort going. They even killed a few to prevent their escape. We all charged into battle, weapons in hand.

I loaded my classic shotgun and started popping first. Once I shot my five shells, I slung the shotgun over my shoulder and pulled out my

SMG, spraying at whatever I could. When I got close enough to the action, I dropped the SMG and started removing heads with my arm blade. Carter was using his strength, throwing men everywhere. He punched so hard, their riot helmets cracked. His armor made him stronger than ever. Genny was quick, rolling and popping helmets off with her rifle. When guards got too close, she pulled out one of her many shivs to shank the men. Kaos had her pistol and katana. The pistol was customized to look like a dragon, and the katana had flowers all over it. She had blood all over her, but she smiled as she mauled the men, enjoying the violence. Once we cleared the guards, it was finally time to go.

As we reached the hole, the warden hopped down from the top of the wall. Carter ran to punch him down, but he dodged it and punched him harder. The warden was wearing the exo suit we'd seen in the blueprints. It knocked Carter down hard. We all ran, but it was too late. The warden let loose his prototype plasma sword  and stabbed Carter right in the neck.

"CARTER!!!" Genny screamed as we reached him, but the warden pushed us all back with a non-lethal blast from his plasma gun.

I stood up, looking at the body. I wanted to be mad, get back to that place of mindless rage, but I couldn't. I remained...

Emotionless.

In one swift motion, I ran toward Warden, dodging all that he could give me. I chopped his arm off and kicked him to the floor. He was screaming. Genny ran over and stabbed the man over and over again in a fit of rage.

The red clouds cleared, showing a momentary blue sky as we stepped out of the prison and looked over the great mass of grass and sand. For the first time in almost a decade, Kaos and Genny experienced the new world. They looked at the landscape, breathing in the air of freedom. Gen fell to her knees, rubbing the tears from her eyes. "Carter...Carter always said he wanted to breathe free air. Now he's free from this world."

I patted her on the shoulder and helped her up. "A good man deserves a burial."

We carried his body and buried it a few yards from the prison. After a few moments of silence, I opened my map. I ripped off part of the Arizona map and gave the rest to Gen and Kaos.

"So, what's next?" I asked.

"H-hey... Genny," Kaos said.

She wiped her eyes. "Yeah?"

"Can we travel together?"

"Sure, Kaos. No problem."

I smiled and hugged both of them.

I stood there for a moment to watch them walk off. I often wondered afterwards, where did they go? What was next for Gen and Kaos?

I watched until the duo turned into specks in the distance before opening my half of the map.

I needed to find my friends.

# CHAPTER FORTY

## RETURN OF DOPEMAN

I walked the desert once again.

I used to feel weak and tired. Now, after all those months of training and fighting, I felt like a new man. I lifted my ripped map, getting a grasp of where I was at. The map covered the area at the entrance of the Grand Canyon National Park. I headed over with the hope that I'd see an ally. As the cold night fell, I heard fighting from afar. Gunfire, screaming, and inhuman sounds. I walked up the sand dune to see a parking lot brawl between the NRF, Desert Demons, and Miller Corps. The lot has seen better days; now it was full of rundown cars, stripped layers of concrete and rubble everywhere. I slid down the dune and ran into the lot. I shot at the Demons and NRF. I didn't have any special rounds, but normal shells still got the job done. I slid into cover behind a car. The Miller Corps guys looked like they'd seen a ghost. I smiled and pulled out my SMG.

After another hour of fighting, the Demons were the only opposing group standing. I was low on ammo, so the arm sword was up to bat. I jumped over the barricade to slice at the tough-skinned lizards. They had spears and knives, but I had to fight. I dispatched four with ease with the help of my arm blade.

The last one kicked me in the chest, knocking me to the ground. The monster held his spear high over his head, ready to kill me. Suddenly, his head was blown to pieces.

I looked up to see Kyle Tann with a smoking gun. Kyle's hand was rusted, but still usable. He had a full beard, and his hair reached his shoulders. He had a new scar over his right eye, most likely due to the Demons.

He looked at me, eyes wide. "Dopeman?!"

I kicked up and ran to hug him. "KYLE! Oh my God, I missed you!"

He hugged me back. It seemed like he needed it. "Me too, it's been Hell out here. Where did you go?"

I let go, sighing. "Long story. You got a camp?"

A trip back to the base later, and I was drinking good water in Kyle's tent. I told him of my jailhouse odyssey. Kyle listened, looking at me the whole time. "Hmm. It explains why you look tougher. And it explains the somewhat new look. But I'm glad you're free."

I scratched my grown out facial hair. "Thanks, Kyle. So, what happened? Where's Sam and Sera?"

He adjusted, sighing. "After the battle of Flagstaff, we lost pretty much everybody. I rounded up as many as I could. Thankfully I found those two, but we couldn't find you. That sandstorm was too rough to turn back, so we had to look for shelter where we were. Then, the Desert Demons attacked. They were ruthless. They kept getting at us. During one fight, a bad sandstorm rushed through. When it stopped, Sera was gone and so were the Desert Demons. We had to push deeper. We found this spot the Demons haven't touched. We've had no word from HQ in Nevada in months. Just when we thought we had it bad, a few days ago NRF joined the fight. Yesterday they captured Fisher. I was terrified. I thought I didn't have the manpower to even save the man. Now that you're here…"

"Yeah. I'll do it. Alone."

Kyle shook his head. "With me, brother."

I shook his hand and smiled.

"About Sera…" Kyle started.

I stopped him. "She's alive. She's in that canyon, I know it. So, what's the plan?"

"We save Fisher, kill the NRF in Arizona, Save Sera, and get to the top of that canyon to find a signal that'll reach Nevada."

I smirked. "I'm in. Got a name for this Op?"

"Operation: Grim Savior."

# CHAPTER FORTY-ONE

## SAVING THE FISHERMAN

With a new boost in morale, we were ready to fight the Desert Demons properly. But first, it was time for our rescue mission. A small group of soldiers volunteered to join in. It was going to be rough, considering the bulk of the NRF was going to be there. We scouted for a day, getting information about the whole camp. It had about twenty people. One of the tents held our target.

Fisher had a bigger beard and a beaten face. Way more handsome look than my shaggy, overgrown look. It appeared he'd been interrogated. It was a bad situation all around.

I was in Kyle's tent the night before the raid, loading up my special shells with some gunpowder Kyle gave me. I was shirtless, and my confidence was through the roof. Kyle was across the tent, tinkering with his rusty arm.

"We go in, guns blazing?" I asked.

He nodded. "We hit them by surprise. We burn the camp down. We kill them all."

I finished stocking up and looked over at him. "Hey, Tann. You ok?"

"Honestly? Not really. Being in the middle of all this can be taxing."

"I'm gonna end this quickly. Take a back seat. I'm gonna lead the charge."

He made a face, but slowly nodded. "I trust you. Don't mess this up, ok?"

"I'm here to kick ass, Tann. Don't worry."

The next morning was gray. The people of the NRF woke up early to get breakfast, freshen up, and get ready for the day. They weren't ready for the pipe bomb thrown in the middle of the camp. The massive explosion dazed some and killed others, and in the confusion we charged in, shooting at the half-dressed soldiers scrambling for cover. I used my SMG to take out the soldiers properly. Once I ran out of ammo, I switched to my shotgun and charged into the camp, making a guard's chest explode with my slug. I ran into the tent behind him to free Fisher. He looked dazed. "D-Dopeman?" He looked to be on the unlucky side of imprisonment. He looked dehydrated.  Bruises all over his neck and torso. He had no shirt, and I could see his ribs poking out.

His legs were basically useless, so I helped him up, half carrying him through other tents to avoid the battle. Eventually, we got near the exit of the camp, but somebody shot at us. I dodged and helped Fisher take cover behind a barrel. I peered over the top of the barrel  to see Godhand, taking out a small pocket of Miller Corpsmen with his machete. Thanks to my big ass hat, he spotted me and ran towards me. I did the same, squeezing my palm to release the blade. We clashed metal, facing off.

Godhand grunted. "Yuh a di scum ah di Earth!"

I pushed him off. "Die!" I attacked, slicing his cheek. He struck back, punching me in the face. I avoided his blade. We fought. The struggle was constant, and only ended with a shot to Godhand's  arm, courtesy of Kyle Tann. Godhand retreated, holding his bloodied arm. I nodded, thanking Kyle as I picked Fisher up. We left the battlefield, burning the camp to the ground. For the first time in a while, Miller Corps gained a major victory.

It felt good.

# CHAPTER FORTY-TWO

## FUTURE SHOCK

I watched Fisher recover slowly. He'd been beaten and not given anything to eat or drink for a few days. I rested with Kyle, using our downtime to drink water and talk about whatever.

"Ever thought of a name for your kid?" I asked one night as we sat around our campfire.

"I was thinking something like Grant. Or Kim if it's a girl."

"What about Dopeman?"

He laughed. "I don't think so, but good try."

I laughed back. "You ever thought about being a father? It must be crazy! A little you."

"In the middle of a war? Not exactly a good environment to have one. My wife hasn't seen me in months, almost a year. I feel so bad for having her miss me for so long."

"Maybe when we get back, you can ask to take a leave. You went toe to toe with Desert Demons and the NRF. That deserves some downtime."

"If we get back."

I patted his back. "Don't talk like that."

The next day, I walked into the medical tent to see Fisher in his bed. "It's Dopeman…" He coughed. "I missed you. I thought I lost two friends."

I took his hand.

He squeezed it, humming. "You got bigger. Hotter too."

I laughed. "Thanks, man. I'm glad you're ok. I'm going to find Sera. Somewhere…" I didn't even know where she even was.

He nodded. "So, where have you been this entire time?"

"Prison. I got captured, like you. What were you questioned about?"

"Hm. No wonder you look tougher. I was just questioned about the location of our HQ. Naturally, I told them to piss off."

I nodded. "Good stuff, my boy. I'll let you recover, I gotta see what Tann has in store next."

"You do that. Good luck kiss?" he joked.

I rolled my eyes playfully and blew him a kiss as I walked out.

I found Kyle loading up a rifle. "Dopeman."

"Oh, how I missed you saying that. Give me the rundown. What's the plan?"

"Ah. I do always say that." He smirked. "Well, today we're gonna raid a park. Roach Mountain National Park. Home to Desert Demons and a piece of tech we need to boost our radio signal so that we can talk to Nevada. All we need to do is to charge in, secure the item, and leave."

I nodded, loading up my Demon Killers. "Sounds like fun. I'm in."

This was a two-man op, so we hiked over to the park alone. We made it there in about two hours. I look at the ruined gates, painted with tribal signs and faces that looked like monsters.  Possibly a way to say keep out. "They can draw now?" I commented.

"They're getting smarter."

"Doesn't matter. They can still die all the same."

# CHAPTER FORTY-THREE

## TOURIST TRAP

We crawled under the bent and destroyed parts of the old gate and walked into the dry park. Dead trees covered the ground, with the sand and dried blood overlapping on the stone path. I readied my shotgun, looking around. "So, what's the device we're looking for?"

Kyle led the way, rifle in hand. "The tool looks like a small piece of metal. The employees here would use these to contact each other across Arizona. The combination of our modifications and the height of the canyon should boost the signal enough to reach HQ. In theory."

"In theory?"

"I know, I know. We don't have a lot of options left. We don't have the supplies to walk back. The helicopters are gone. With your help, we can get out of here in one piece."

I agreed. As we reached the visitor's center, I noticed more Demon markings. It was almost like a story. A tale of their upbringing, their evolution. The center had a shrine to what must've been their god. "We're heading into a place of worship," Tann commented.

I chuckled. "Just don't blow it up this time."

"Ha. No promises."

We stepped inside to see a room full of human corpses. Their chests were cut open, hearts removed. The people and  floors were marked with paint and blood, and the walls were messily painted with cloud marks. I shook my head. "They're sacrificing people."

Kyle looked in disbelief. "These all look fresh. From Miller Corps and NRF."

"I knew they sacrificed, but this much?"

"We got a study that says they sacrifice in times of danger. We purposely sabotaged a tribe's water supply, and they took our lookouts for sacrifice to their gods. We saved them, of course. If they're taking this many people, it must be bad. Real bad."

Something clicked in my head as I checked a body. "Wait, you said that the day Sera disappeared she was fighting Demons, right?"

"Yeah..."

I hit the table in frustration. I needed to get into that canyon. Now.

As I headed for the exit, Demons burst through the door. Some used makeshift bows to shoot arrows at us. We dove for  cover, shooting back. I used my Demon Killers to blow their bodies apart. Kyle popped at the monsters, killing them. We ran when we saw an opening, pushing through the lizards to run out of the visitor's center and down the trail. We shot at them as we sprinted. Green stained the ground. Kyle and I rushed through the foliage, running across the park. We eventually found the Insect Center, a smaller area for employees. There were no windows, and just one door.

*Perfect*

We kicked in the door and slammed it shut, using an old vending machine to barricade it. I looked around as the Demons slammed against the door. "Cover me. I'll find the thing." Kyle nodded and aimed at the door.

It was cracking under the strain of bodies. Demon hands broke through the aging door.  Kyle opened fire. I ran into an employee break room. Desert Demon bodies had been abandoned here to decay in the open air. I also saw a large, red 'X' with some scribbles under it. I wished I could read Demon. The place was a mess, so I moved bodies and tables out of the way to find what I was looking for. I found supplies, but no device until I upended a dusty box on a rotting table. Signal boosters tumbled out. They were all destroyed. I rooted through to find the only one that wasn't damaged. I took that, along with the supplies, and ran out to see Kyle stabbing and shooting the Demons. I threw my flashbang to stun them, picked Kyle up and ran to the emergency trail. We crawled through a small crack in the fence, too small for the Demons to follow us. After running for a while, it was finally safe enough to stop for a break. I set down the box, panting.

Kyle looked at the box. "Did you..."

I pulled out the booster. "Yeah."

# CHAPTER FORTY-FOUR

## MOP THEM UP

The Miller Corps engineers examined the booster. One of them finally spoke up. "It's a decent piece. We can upgrade it, but we need a few days to modify it properly."

Kyle nodded. "How many days is a few days?"

"It depends, sir. We'll let you know."

I walked out, letting them talk. I spotted Fisher and went up to him. We walked together. "You doing ok, Dopeman?" he asked.

I shook my head. "I'm worried. What if we're too late? What if Sera is…"

Sam put his hand up. "Come on, man. We got this. Say, while I was captured, I got this rumor about a Shaman. They say he speaks to Demons. He understands them. A small group of men left camp to hunt for him."

"You tryna cheer me up with tall tales?" I chuckled. "Where is this Shaman? Gives us a good excuse to bust some heads."

"Over at Lake Retals. One of the shack houses they said."

"Sounds like fun. let's do it!"

We told Kyle and he gave us a green light to go. At the same time, A scout team went out in the opposite direction  to the Grand Canyon.

We had a bit of fun walking over to the lake, playing I spy.

"I spy with my little eye, something..." Fisher looked around for a moment. "White!"

I groaned. "Dude, It's bones. You said that like five times already."

Fisher rolled his eyes. "Oh? You want me to say sand and rocks three more times?"

 Soon we reached the lake. It was black. Lightning struck its glassy surface. I grunted. "That lake looks disgusting."

"Well, welcome to Arizona. This place sucks."

"You could've said that ten years ago."

We laughed as we headed over to the lake houses. There were rows of them, all indistinguishable from each other except for one. The NRF had made camp around that house. One of them banged on the door. "We need that information, Shaman! If you don't comply, we're going to use force."

That was our chance. Sam shot the doorman while I shot my AP rounds at the camp. I killed two of the men coming out of a tent. Then I ran forward and drove my shoulder into someone's chest, knocking him down. One tried to get me from behind, but I dodged and cut his throat with my blade. As the last one got up, Fisher popped him in the head. I gave him a thumbs up.

We walked up to the shack and looked at the door. "Hello? Shaman?" I spoke. "We're not..."

The door opened. We walked in.

"The DOPEMAN can come. The FISHERMAN can stay."

We looked shocked. How did he know our names?

"I'll stay. Good luck, Dopeman."

I'd need it.

# CHAPTER FORTY-FIVE

## SHAMAN'S TRAIL

I walked through the old lake house, taking in the chipped wood floorboards, the fading wallpaper. I felt an odd sensation. I was leaving this world, almost. I walked into a room that held a man in ragged clothes. One of his eyes was green, and the other brown. He had tattoos similar to the Demon markings I'd seen at Roach Mountain National park. He turned to me. "The DOPEMAN." He had a deep booming voice. It was almost inhuman. "Sit."

I slowly sat down. "How do you know my name?"

"The SPIRITS."

"And what are these spirits?

"The SPIRITS are the SPIRITS."

I rolled my eyes. "As long as these spirits can help me."

Shaman shook his head. "I require a TEST. The RIGHTEOUS men desire to CONTROL the SPIRITS. Will you do the same?"

"No. All I need is their help. I'll take your test. What is it, algebra or something?"

He laughed. "Comedy from the DOPEMAN. The SPIRITS told your story. A tale of a man who sold POISON to your hometown. It filled you with a head of guilt and a heart of loneliness. Now you want to redeem yourself by DELIVERING items."

"Uh…Yeah. So, what's this test?"

Shaman handed me a pipe. I held it in my hand and looked at it. It looked familiar. There was no way it could be what I thought it was…

"You sold the POISON to your town, but have you ever tasted the POISON?" he asked.

I knew it. It was crack. He'd spiked it, too. Laced it with something. Hopefully, it wouldn't kill me. I grabbed his lighter and smoked. As I coughed the smoke, I felt…

***

Wrong.

The room started to fall apart.

Shaman laughed and chanted something. He was performing some ritual. I look around to see a gray void, almost cloud-like. It was storming, lightning and thunder. I stood. I looked down to see my lack of weapons. All I had was my arm blade. Desert Demons popped suddenly from the ground, ready to strike. They had eyes of flame. Skin of lava. I started running. Running far away. I tripped and fell. As I got up, I saw my mother.

"What's wrong?" she asked. "I thought you had forgotten everything? I thought you went to church? I thought you forgave yourself?"

You're not real.

"I'm very real, [**REDACTED**]. Oops! I said your name. You're the Dopeman now, right."

You left me. You made me like this.

"You left me to fend for myself. Your own mother. Shame on you—"

Don't say my name.

"What? Still on that, boy? Nobody cares about you. You're the Dopeman. that's it."

I'm more than that.

"Then what are you?"

*I... I am...*

"What? What?"

Suddenly, my mother's face melted into another Desert Demon. I squeezed my palm and cut its head off. I bled lava. I started chopping and killing all I could. I was going mad. But I had to. I had to keep pushing. The bodies around me started to decay. I felt weak.

I fell to my knees.

All the thoughts of lust, the hunger for power. I was a bad man. I knew that. And I forgave myself. I promised I wouldn't do it. I would be a servant to the people.

Dopeman. The Foolish Courier.

The room started to re-form. I passed out.

***

I woke up to find the Shaman staring at me. "The SPIRITS spoke to you." He pulled out the ashes to sniff them.

"Did you make me smoke ashes?"

"YES."

I made a face and sat up. "How long was I out?"

"TIME has no meaning in the land of—"

"Cut it before I stuff the spirits down your throat."

"Twenty minutes."

I made a smug face. "Good. Since I passed the test, I need you to answer some questions."

"Speak."

"The Demons, why are they taking so many people away?"

The Shaman threw some ash in the air, humming. "They are sick. They CONSUME the waste of angels, they believe it to be something divine. They are WRONG. It makes them sick. it turns into a virus, making them decay from the inside."

I tilted my head. "So, they're using sacrifices to get rid of the plague."

He nodded.

"How do I stop this?"

"Crush the TRIBE."

I was confused. "What?"

He stayed silent. I stood up. "How do you know Demon, Shaman?"

"Simple. I put my faith in the SPIRITS."

"Sure. I'll see you around, pal."

He hummed a song and threw more ash. Weird guy.

I walked outside to Fisher. "Got any information?" he asked.

"We'll walk and talk."

I explained everything on the way back. As we reached the camp, Fisher grunted. "Bout time something bad happened to them. But there might be more of that sickness in the canyon. Watch yourself."

I gave him a fist bump before walking to Kyle's tent to explain everything.

"You're going to believe a man who smokes ashes?" he asked.

"Pretty much."

"Huh. Well, ignore that. Got word that we found one more pocket of NRF."

"Oh yeah? Then let's go!" I yelled.

# CHAPTER FORTY-SIX

## END OF AN ERA

Sera was heavy on my mind. The scouting team had yet to return from the Grand Canyon. To make things worse, my arm blade was getting dull. I sharpened it using an old stone. A sandstorm raged outside, so I couldn't do much else. Kyle walked in, holding a fire ax. He sat with me. "Something's on your mind?"

"Sera. I'm really worried."

"Listen, Dopeman. If we're too late…"

"I know. It's just nice to think there's a chance she's alive."

"I understand. But there was something else. I got a memo this morning. From Godhand. He wants to fight you one-on-one to settle the score. For everything."

"Everything?"

"Yup. You win, we can have all of his men. They will pledge under Miller Corps. If he wins, we'll do the opposite."

"Why me? You're the commander, Kyle. I'm just a courier."

"Stop lying to yourself. You're Dopeman. You're the face of this operation. All anybody can talk about is you."

I looked down, remembering all I'd done. "I'm pretty cool ain't I?"

He chuckled and passed me the ax. "Yeah. Now he said hand weapons only, no guns. If you want to accept, here."

I nodded. "I won't disappoint."

As he left, I got an idea I remembered from old-world advertisements. A certain ax that emitted plasma. I nabbed a few wires and laced the live wires with plasma from old LED lights. It was unstable, but with a shake, it worked. With everything set up, I headed to bed early.

The next day we met Godhand near a sinkhole. A new sandstorm was brewing, and I had my face covered. It was clear that Godhand wasn't gonna wait for better weather. Neither was I. Fisher was next to me, holding my guns while I stared at the enemy. Godhand held two machetes. The crowd formed a circle with us in the middle, similar to the prison fight. Kyle was behind me, rubbing my shoulders. "Remember, this man put you in jail for months. He's the reason you left us."

I hopped in the air and huffed. The Miller Corps men yelled encouragement. Godhand laughed. "Dis is the man. The man who ruined di Miller Corps. This was a mistake."

I shook the fire ax, and it popped out a purple light. "Enough talk. I wanna mount your head on a spear."

He shook his machetes to emit an orange plasma. "Yuh nah guh survive! Yuh a guh bi fed tuh di demons!"

He charged with an overhead strike. I blocked with the ax handle and pushed him off. I went for a swipe at his midsection, but he moved and cut with his blade. I felt a burning slice on my cheek. I backed away, but he was on the attack, going for massive swings at my head. I ducked out the way and his machetes hit the sand. Godhand jumped over my ax as I attacked his legs. I hopped up and attempted to disarm him, but he cut my side. I fell to my knees and he swung for my neck. I chopped off his right arm as quickly as I could. He yelled. I saw that as an opportunity to chop at this man like a tree. I cut a leg off. He was on the floor; the NRF quieted and I heard my men yell out, "DOPEMAN! DOPEMAN! DOPEMAN!"

I aimed at his neck. He grunted. "Deh will bi more. Yuh cyaan tap freedom."

I chopped his head clean off and picked it up by the dreads. I raise it to the NRF. "Welcome to Miller Corps! We appreciate your service."

# CHAPTER FORTY-SEVEN

## ENTER THE CANYON

After the fight, we gathered all of the men and walked back to camp. The NRF were men of their word, I'll admit that. It was awkward at first, seeing the enemy remove their old armor. Removing their past and donning new armor with the Miller Corps patch.

The soldiers decided to celebrate the end of the Arizona conflict with a party. We moved and grooved, dancing to the beat some old NRF soldiers made using containers and buckets. I indulged myself and drank some booze.

I was a really light drinker.

I was on my first glass of wine when I sat down with a former NRF soldier. She had nice dreads and a good smile. "It's the Dopeman."

I made myself comfortable. "Yes, It's me. And you are?"

"Call me Mox."

"Nice name. You like the camp?"

"Yeah, It's cool. I love the environment. You people seem alright. Though it will be weird to just. Fight for you."

"Why even join the NRF in the first place?"

Mox shrugged. "I like freedom. I thought the war would be over by now, but he kept dragging us. This is the first time in a while I sat down, drank some good stuff. Actually talked."

"Geez, they're strict."

"Maybe that's true. We were machines though. Getting things done quickly."

I nodded and downed the rest of the wine.

One glass turned to three. I was gone at that point. I don't remember much, just a lot of dancing, beat playing, and kissing. Who? Good question.

I woke up to a sudden rush of water. I gasped and looked up to see an annoyed Kyle. "Rise and shine. Scout team came back." He walked away, whistling. I looked around to see Fisher and Mox next to me, groaning awake.

I hated drinking.

I got some water and walked over to Kyle's tent. The three-man scout team leaned on the table, smoking. "The legend,." their leader said. He was covered in blood. He also had a British accent.

"Nice to meet ya," I said. "So, what's the deal?"

"I'll keep it short. The area is enclosed and covered in dead bodies. It's also impossible for even a three-man team. I'm afraid in order to boost that signal, you'll need one man to do it. Also, no guns. If you shoot, the entire tribe will hear. It's better to sneak around."

Kyle and I took in the information.

I raised my hand. "I'll go."

Kyle patted my back. "Not like I can change your mind."

I sobered up and grabbed my ax.

I was starting to leave when Fisher grabbed my shoulder. "Dopeman, please come back." He moved to peck me on the lips.

"Uh...Sure!" I got confused. What the hell happened last night? While I didn't mind it, that was my first kiss with a man. Was it even romantic? I didn't have time to think about my sexuality, so I smiled and continued my walk over to the entrance of the canyon. It was marked with more Demon scribbles. It had a red mist around it.

I walked in.

*Here I come, Sera.*

# CHAPTER FORTY-EIGHT

## KING OF THE DEMONS, PART ONE

The Grand Canyon National Park. An Arizona tourist attraction. It used to be miles of beautiful landscapes. Now it was a death trap. The origin of the Desert Demons. It was haunting. For the first time, I was worried about the future. It was too late now to leave; I needed to push in.

As I stepped into the rocky canyon, the red mist got worse. It was coming from the bodies of humans and Demons. They'd been killing so many people so frequently in this packed environment, the blood was almost in the air, smelling of iron and rotting corpses. The blood felt like fog on a rainy day. It made me sick to my stomach. The walls and ground were marked with simple stick figure art. As I advanced, the bodies piled up more and more. Their ages varied from bones to freshly cut open. Was Sera among those bodies? I snuck up to one of the piles, tossing bodies aside and looking at their disfigured faces. Miller Corps, NRF, and some prisoners from the breakout were there. I wondered how many they caught. I didn't see Sera, so I set a corpse down and resumed sneaking.

I also saw bars in carved-out sections of the canyon. It was a prison. Two were empty, so no saving them this time. I kept on the trail, walking with my ax. I spotted two Demons walking towards me. Thanks to the blood mist they couldn't see me. I hid behind a rock. I waited till they passed me, then I remembered my plasma and threw the ax at one. It struck the Demon dead. As it fell, I ran toward the other one with my arm blade, but it caught my wrist. It threw me to the ground. The Demon tried to end the fight early with a spear thrust. I rolled to my right and stabbed it in the arm. It gushed green as I pulled out the blade. They must have a high pain tolerance, because it rushed me, stabbing me in the leg. I screamed as my thigh gushed blood. I stumbled to my feet and ran to my ax, toughing it out. I blocked the spear with the ax handle. I rolled my ax to drive it into its neck. Green blood spilled out. It stopped moving, but I started to chop at its side, making deeper cuts. I eventually split it in half. It started raining green. I sighed.

I grabbed the two spears, broke the sticks, and removed the ropes holding the spear tips. I tied the points around the end of my ax, making a thrusting end for it. Gave me some new options. I did a few thrusts to test it out. I liked it.

I could test my new modification on two more Demons coming up on me, chanting as they walked. As the first Demon reached me I thrust my spear end into its midsection, ruining its guts. The second quickly rallied and tried to attack, but I used the first Demon's body as a shield, making it stab its comrade in the chest. I kicked both of them down. One of them stood up, however. It grabbed both of the spears to attack me. I moved out of the way out of multiple attacks. I spun and kicked the monster in the chest, knocking it to the floor. I finished the injured one off with an ax slam, smashing its face in. I turned to end the other with my bladed arm. I pulled it off. I was sweating and breathing hard, grimacing at the pain of my injured leg. These were some tough beasts.

I learned some new things about these people, that was for sure. They had a high pain tolerance and a lot of blood inside them. My clothes already had a high mix of green and red stains. After catching my breath, I went back to the trail. The path grew narrower, with rocks surrounding me. I squeezed through the rocks, and came out into another open area. There were three paths. To the east and west, I saw only desert, with a weak wooden gate blocking the path west. There was a mountain-like peak to the north. The sky above the peak was red, and lightning struck the peak. I'd found my target. I pulled out my hand radio and checked the booster. I hoped it worked. But first, I was curious to see how many people had been captured. I started to sneak along the northern path when I heard a human voice. "Psst! Dopeman!" I turned to see some strange man, captured. He was tied to a pole. "Dopeman! Help!"

I turned and got closer. It was the Ant. This got better and better.

I walked up to him, chuckling. "What a surprise. Hello, Ant."

He scoffed. "Can you let me down? Why are you just looking at me?!"

"I mean, It's a little funny."

"No, it's not! Now let me down!"

I inspected the pole he was tied to. It wasn't trapped, so I shrugged and cut him down. He fell and hit the ground with a thud. I cut him free fully. He stood up and grabbed my shirt.

"Listen, Dopeman. The rest of the people need help!"

I looked confused. "Like, the rest of your crew is here? What happened?"

"After the breakout, we were all lost as hell. We ain't grab a map so we wandered right into the hands of the Desert Demons. It was bad. Some of us got taken to be sacrificed. I'm so pissed! I can't wait to get my hands on them!" His body shook with anger.

"Huh. Well, I think you need to think this through. You're not gonna kill all of them all by yourself."

"That's why I have you! You're gonna help me! Come on! I need this!"

I put my hands up. "Don't guilt-trip me... Fine. I'll help you. Just make it quick, I'm looking for somebody."

"Who?" he asked.

"A woman. Blonde hair. Has a lot of muscle. Know who that is?"

The small man shook his head. "No. I've been out here for a while."

The Ant started walking and I followed. "And where are the other prisoners?"

"The Eastern path, come on!"

Guess the rescue mission got a whole lot bigger.

# CHAPTER FORTY-EIGHT (PART II)

## KING OF THE DEMONS, PART TWO

I followed the Ant onto the eastern path. On the way to the prisoner camp, we saw a small group of Demons. We hid behind a rock, watching four monsters. Once again, the Demons had spears and plenty of armor on their bodies. I looked over to the Ant. "You need a weapon. We're gonna attack those dudes."

He made a face. "And how would we do that? Not like I have a weapon now."

I picked up a medium-sized rock and handed it to him. "Good luck!" I charged the nearest Demon, driving my ax into its neck. The Ant followed and bashed the second Demon in the head with his rock, making the beast fall. The Ant charged another monster, mounting it and bashing its head in ruthlessly. Seemed like he was attempting to get his anger out. The fourth Demon was trying to stab the Ant in the back, but I intercepted it by chopping at its leg. The wound gushed green as the Demon collapsed, and I finished it off with a swing to the dome. Once all the creatures were dead, I grabbed a spear. "Here's your weapon. You're welcome."

He grabbed the spear and inspected it, checking how sharp it was. "This might be enough."

I pointed to one of the bodies. "Pick up the armor, too."

"Ew, you expect me to put that on? That's weird."

I passed him the armor. "Beggars can't be choosers."

Ant reluctantly equipped himself, getting ready for the battle ahead of us.

We continued on the eastern path, seeing a lot more prisoners. None of them had made it. . Eventually, I saw a trail of men and women held captive, waiting for sacrifice. Of course, these people were no longer alive. The cells were a blood bath. The inside of the cells were marked. I assumed the signs meant danger or something. "These people are dead…" I mumbled, horrified.

"Yup," Ant said. "These are just the ones who resisted. They tried to rebel like you, and it ended in failure."

I shook my head, angered by the sight of more of the dead in this cruel place. "How did you end up at the front?"

"Uhh… I guess they didn't consider me worthy? I don't know. Nor do I care. Shh! My boys are in those cells."

I saw a lot of my former opponents in cells, waiting. Okuda was walking behind his bars. He looked at the Demons with anger. A lot of Demons were guarding the area. I'd seen enough. "Here's the plan. We go in, kill, open up the cells, and have them run. Sounds good?"

He nodded.

"It's showtime!" I ran down the trail, kicking up the plasma and cutting a head clean off. I moved out of the way of two spears from two Demons and broke them with my feet. I drove my ax into one of their chests and killed the other with a blade to its neck. My face got splattered with green as I pulled away. I retrieved my ax as three more came up to me. I thrust the spear-tipped end into a Demon's stomach, as another Demon stabbed my right arm. Another came up from behind, but I pulled the spear up, jumped to kick the one behind me, and shanked the beast on my right in the throat multiple times. It dropped dead. I gave it a kick for good measure. I looked over, watching Ant do his thing as he freed his friends.

The Ant drove his spear right into a Demon's throat and the Okuda picked up a club to bash a lizard's head in. They were a good duo, fighting and killing plenty of Demons. They took turns cutting down their opponents as quickly as possible while the other guarded them. I ran and used the distractions as an opportunity to free the rest of the prisoners. It soon turned to a full-on riot, prisoners brawling with the Desert Demons. So much for the quiet approach. It was so loud, it echoed through the entire canyon. I joined the fight, using my ax to claim some heads myself. I was cutting and getting cut myself in the heavy contest of the brawl.

After the fight, the prisoners began  arming themselves with the weapons of their dead enemies. I climbed up to a platform to see one last cell. I broke it open to see another man, sitting down. He was weak, so I helped him up. "Geez, how long have you been there?"

"Months," he answered. His voice was gruff and he sounded older.

"Geez... How did you survive for so long?"

The stranger coughed and grabbed a stick for help. His face was hidden with a hood. "They forget us sometimes. They just throw raw meat at us. These monsters keep no records or tapes. They only take and kill."

I sighed as he limped after me. "Say, did you happen to see a blonde girl around here?"

He shook his head. "Your best chances are the western trail, but that's all I know. But there will be a lot of resistance over there. Especially after what you did here."

I walked to the edge and looked at the masses of prisoners. All of them were angry and confused. They didn't want to run into the unknown again. "I'm gonna need help. YO!"

The prisoners turned to me. I put my hands out. "I'm not gonna lie to you, this is dangerous. You can leave, wander the desert till the hunger gets ya, or you can take revenge on these monsters! You can RISE UP! BECOME THE DEMON SLAYERS!"

The men yelled, raising their weapons to pledge their arms to me. "DOPEMAN! DOPEMAN! DOPEMAN!"

"Good! NOW LET'S BUST SOME HEADS!"

# CHAPTER FORTY-NINE

## KING OF THE DEMONS, PART THREE

This was supposed to be a one-man mission.

It was supposed to be simple.

Now it was an eighty-man war. I was in charge of an army in the blink of an eye. We charged the small, weak gates of the western trail. We used our overwhelming numbers to break down the feeble wall. At first the trail was unguarded, but Demons crawled out of their holes and ran down the path to fight us. I was on the front lines, chopping off limbs with my plasma ax and fighting hard to win the day. Our army was at a standstill with the Demons. I needed to help turn the tide. I ran off the trail into a shack that looked like an old gift shop. I saw two Demons run after me. I had an idea, so I kept on the chase. They drew closer, almost close enough to hook their claws in the back of my coat. I turned on a dime to cut the first monster in half, swinging my mighty ax like a baseball bat. I should've gotten into sports back in the day.

The other Demon had a bone sword. He was quick, but I was quicker. I dodged slices and deflected thrusts. Once I got a proper deflect that left him open, I rammed the spear end into his neck. I turned it to the side and pushed, opening his throat. I chopped at his head to finish him. He was a bloody mess when I was done. Then I ran into the shack and looked around until I saw what I needed to step up the fight: containers full of Angel Waste.

I covered my mouth as I looked inside. It was a more solid form, like the Waste the NRF made in a barrel. Must be the last batch. I looked around the gift shop to see bottles of booze, plenty of them. Seeing them gave me an idea. I snatched the bottles off the counter and emptied them, then scooped the Waste into the bottles and stoppered them with rags. The unstable substance reacted violently as I shook the bottle. It should be enough to get rid of them, but not too harmful for breathing. I took six bottles and ran to the battlefield, ready to save the day.

I climbed up the rocks overlooking the fight. I turned and chucked the four glass bottles, one at a time, aiming at the rear of the Demon ranks. The white puff exploded all over the battlefield, burning and eating the Demons. It hurt a few prisoners, too, and some died for the sake of victory.

However, that was the turning point for my boys. The men pushed through, making it a bloodbath for the monsters. I smiled. We were going to win.

I caught an arrow in the shoulder. I fell a few feet, and my head bounced off the rocky ground below. It knocked me out cold for who knows how long.

WhenI snapped awake, my head throbbed in pain and my ears were ringing. Once the world stopped spinning, I tried pulling the arrow out. The first few tugs only made the point sink deeper into my wound, but at last I was able to get the arrow out. I bled a lot, yelling in pain. I gritted my teeth, holding my shoulder as my clothes stained red. I had to continue the fight, so I had to get up.

I used a piece of my cape to wrap my injured shoulder as we charged the tight spaces on the western trail. This path was a lot bloodier. The mist was thick, and held the sick corpses of the Demons and more sacrificed people. The cells multiplied. It was also darker. The sky was covered by a red fog. We ignored it and freed more prisoners, killing the Demons in small pockets as we came upon them. They refused to retreat, so they paid the ultimate price. We kept up the pressure. It was obvious that we were gonna win this fight.

I saw a big cell as we headed into the center of the prison complex. I walked up, only to see a smaller Demon with double daggers charging at me. I tried to swing at it, but my arm was killing me. It drove its daggers into my sides. I dropped the ax and fell to the ground. The Demon pulled out and tried to stab my chest, but I kicked it off, kicked up, and tossed my fifth bottle of waste. It blocked with its arm, and the waste sprayed over its skin, wasting and rotting it in a matter of seconds. I took advantage of the distraction and stabbed the freak in the head. Grassy blood gushed over my hand. In frustration, I continued punching, destroying the head and neck as I finished off the brute. I coughed, leaned on the rocks, dragging myself to open the cells and saw...

*Sera.*

She was on the floor, wasting away. The room was covered in blood, with a few dead Demons beside her. She was clinging to life. I fell next to her, holding her head.

"Hey..." she said quietly. I looked down. She'd been stabbed. She'd been bleeding out for a while. My eyes moved rapidly, looking her over as I started to shake.  I was trying to think of what to do, anything. I didn't want to say goodbye. I didn't want to see her go.

She coughed weakly. "No tears... Please."

I shook my head. "How c-can I not cry? You're gonna..."

She put her bloody finger to my lips. I broke down and held her close. "It's not your fault, Dopeman. You did all this f-for me..."

"Always. I'll do so much for you, Sera." I said. "I can't. I won't..."

She grunted. "Remember when you told me the story of Dani's death? How didn't you say goodbye?"

I looked at her, the tears falling off my chin. "G-Goodbye... Sera. I love you."

"I love you too, Dopeman..."

She wiped my tears away. I kissed her one last time. She started to tear up as well.

We sat in silence for a few minutes. I closed my eyes, resting with her. Her feeble attempts to breathe broke my heart. After a few minutes of slow, pained breathing, she stopped.

"Sera..." I whispered.

No response.

"Sera... Sera..." I looked down. She was gone. I shook, beginning to break down..

At least I was able to say goodbye.

At least I was able to say goodbye.

# CHAPTER FIFTY
## KING OF THE DEMONS, PART FOUR

I stopped with the tears, eventually, and rested my head on the dirty walls. I still held her in my arms. I'd failed again. I didn't even know if I could even call for help. I pulled out the hand radio, staring at it. How could I complete this mission? How could I get this job done? How could I do anything anymore? I was so lost.

In my haze of emotions, I saw...

*Me?*

I saw a phantom-like version of me. He looked younger, less stressed. He didn't have the messy stubble. He still had a twinkle in his eye. He sat with me. He seemed content. Deep in thought. "Hey," he said.

I shook my head, confused. "What? Have I gone fully insane?"

The phantom laughed. "No, no. Well, sort of. I'd say this is your brain defending itself. We seem to be in a bad way."

I smiled. "Ah. You're talking about this, aren't you?"

"Yeah. You're gonna give up on the mission, just rot here."

"Well, I'm tired of failure. I'm tired of losing."

Phantom adjusted himself, thinking about what to say next. "Remember when Kyle lost his arm?"

"How could I forget?"

"In my eyes, we get hurt to learn something or get stronger. I can't say to the pain you're feeling, but I can say you're not alone, Kyle. You have people here for you."

The phantom stood. "Follow your own advice."

"But how can I get this done? I'm just gonna fail. Somebody's gonna die. I'm gonna screw this up."

"We do it our own way. You know what to do, win or lose you do it your way. " He disappeared.

Yeah. I thought I did know what to do. I gave Sera one last kiss and set her down. I'd retrieve the body later.

I walked outside to see my prison army, even bigger and waiting for me. They chanted and cheered for me. I grabbed my ax and put my hands up, angry and determined. "People! The time for revenge is almost upon us. I want us on that northern trail! I want Demon heads on the ground! I WANT BLOOD! DO YOU WANT BLOOD?!"

The crowd chanted. "HELL YES!"

"WHOSE BLOOD YOU WANT?"

"DEMONS! DEMONS! DEMONS!"

I smiled, shaking my ax to emphasize my words. "Then let's claim some heads!"

We ran to the wall of the northern trail. It was heavily fortified, with a massive wooden gate to keep us from advancing. There were Demons in front of us, threatening us with spears, ready to fight back. The Demons were also on top of the walls, shooting sharp arrows down at us. They were getting good shots off as well, killing or injuring quite a few of us. I had to cut the men in front of us. I used the arm blade to cut and kill the monstrosities in front of me. Once I got them out of the way, I ordered some men to start climbing. I needed to let off steam, so I joined the climbing team. We headed up the walls. Some got hit with the arrows, falling into the bloody mosh pit below. A few lucky ones, including me, made it up.

We climbed over the top and started fighting. I tried to shake my plasma, but it sparked and sputtered and didn't come out. I'd have to do it the hard way. That was fine, I wanted to get all my anger out anyways. I hit the first monster I saw right in the skull with my ax. I pulled out the ax and started wildly swinging at the green freaks. I was yelling like a mad man. I felt as though l was in the World Series. The other Demons tried to stop me, but I was in the zone. I broke their spears with my ax and finished some off with my arm sword. I brutally stabbed them in the heart or neck, covering myself in filth as I fought on the strong wooden wall. I turned my ax to the spear end, opening the stomachs and throats of the beasts. The men soon rallied around me and fought with me. I yelled in celebration as we took them out. The army yelled back in the adrenaline rush. We got down as we used our numbers to bring the wooden gates down. I stepped in front, keeping the bloodied, angry prisoners at bay.

"Now. You want blood. I want blood. They killed your friends, your family. They ripped their hearts out for this!" I pointed at the markings, the tribal signs. The prisoners yelled and chanted. "I WANT DEAD DEMONS ON THE GROUND. DO YOU WANT THAT TOO?!"

The men overwhelmingly yelled, "YEAH!!"

"Great. CHARGE!"

We all ran into the northern trail.

The heart of the Desert Demons.

# CHAPTER FIFTY-ONE

## KING OF THE DEMONS, PART FIVE

There was a storm brewing. The gray clouds grumbled and lightning flashed in the sky. I thought it was gonna be sand or some form of Angel Waste, but it was...

Rain.

It started to rain. We all looked in the sky, shocked. I had to shake it off; we needed to advance quickly. "MEN!" I yelled as we cleared the gate. "The rain is a sign. We must strike! Go!" We charged down the trail, keeping our spirits high as we ran down the path.

We saw what must be the main camp. A line of Demons with spears separated us from the archers, shooting a volley of arrows. Many of us fell, but we hit the camp soon. It was another battle, with both sides deep in the contest. I was in the middle of it all, fighting.

I saw some Demons cutting down and killing the prisoners. I saw the prisoners hurt and cut the Demons. We hit and brutalized each other, making sure we didn't go down under the harsh strikes, hurtful cuts, and bashes. I kept up the tempo, brawling with the Demons while pushing forward. I was caked in green and red, using my ax to claim these monster's lives. My own body bled from multiple cuts and bruises. I kept the battle going. The Demons tried to keep their momentum, but to no avail. We kept it pushing to the center of the camp, leaving a trail of bodies behind us.

As we reached a bonfire, I saw four marked Demons, ready to attack. I moved out of the way of the first spear attack. I threw my ax at the second Demon, killing it. Then I grabbed the first monster and slit its throat. Two more tried to stab me at the same time. I used the corpse of the dead Demon as a meat shield, hopped back, and chucked the last bottle of Angel Waste at the two, killing them. As I landed, I collapsed in pain. As I got up, and got my ax back,  more Demons tried to attack me. I rolled out of the way and put the ax to one of their legs. I hopped on his neck and started thrusting my arm blade into the wretched best. I struck until it stopped moving. Then I grabbed the ax from its legs and chopped at its neck until it was severed.

I panted as I looked past the rain. My face was covered in rainwater for the first time in over a decade. I opened my mouth. It tasted wonderful. I grabbed a few rocks at the bottom of the mountain and started to climb.

I was taking my time, being careful not to slip and fall. I slowly climbed up to a small platform. I thought I could use that as a resting area on the way down. The rain felt nice, at least. Lightning struck all over the mountain, the wind was strong, and the rain was heavy. I was halfway there when I felt scales around my waist. Something heavy grabbed my waist and pulled me off the mountainside, sending the both of us flying, I lost my ax on the way down. I hit a high platform back-first, gasping and losing my breath. I slowly got up, panting, and saw a massive Desert Demon. He must've been the chief. He was strong, and stood taller than most humans. He had piercings and tattoos on his face and chest.

He smiled and cracked his knuckles. "Furgap. Garr!"

I held my fists up. I was gonna take him down myself. I went aggressive and attempted to punch him in the gut. He took it with no effort and put his knee to my stomach. He punched me to the floor. I stumbled up and started to go for rapid strikes and kicks. He blocked them all. He was invincible. He wasn't fazed by a single hit I threw at him. Constantly, he threw them to the side. If I just kept up the punching and kicking—

He caught my fist and threw me aside with ease. I was getting frustrated. What did I need to do?

Wait, I'm playing his game, I thought. All my fights, all my victories, I played my way. That was why I lost to Kaos. I played on her terms. With this in mind, I charged. I dodged his hook and unleashed my arm blade, sending it right up his side. Chief wasn't expecting that. He bled more and more as I sent more punches his way. I poked hole after hole in his scaled body. I grabbed his shoulder and ruthlessly drove my blade in his gut. With one final punch to the face, he fell flat, bleeding out and crawling away. I walked up to him and grabbed his head. I put the blade to his neck and started sawing his head off, making sure the crowd saw. I drove the blade in,staining the platform as I sawed deeper and deeper. The Demonswere shocked at my act of violence, and stopped the fight to look at me. I yelled as I pulled off his head. The Demons and prisoners paused in horror. Hundreds had their eyes on me, gripping the head of the strongest monster in the canyon.

All I could do was yell.

Yell in frustration, relief.

The Demons bowed suddenly.

The king is dead. Long live the king.

I tossed the head on the ground and started to climb the slick rocks as the rain stopped. The journey felt as long as the canyon war. I was hurt, I was tired from all that fighting. But I pushed onward to the top.

I reached the top. I brought out  the radio. It was cracked, but working. I pressed the button. "Hello, HQ? This is Dopeman!"

Static.

"Please... Pick up! HQ! HQ!"

Static.

"No... Damn it!"

Static. "Hello? This is Green, over."

"Thank God! We're in Arizona! We need back up, ASAP."

"Got it. Send the cords and we'll be there soon."

Mission complete.

# CHAPTER FIFTY-TWO

## DEMON CLASS OF 2093

I gave Green the coordinates.

"Got it. We'll be there in approximately three weeks," Green said. As I gathered my strength, I took my hat off and placed my head on the rocks. I closed my eyes. I felt myself starting to relax. For once, I could sleep.

At that moment, I felt a weight lifted from my shoulders. I didn't care that I was so high up. I didn't care that I was this close to falling into the depths below.

I opened my eyes to get the scope of the land. The destroyed landscapes and the sand. I breathed out, feeling the cold air on my face. I could almost cry.

Eventually, I climbed down. My legs gave out as I landed. I laughed to myself. It was finally over. I slumped to the ground and closed my eyes.

I was out for who knows how long. I was poked awake by a Demon. "Gruap?" it said.

I yelled, scooting away. It stared at me blankly and tilted its head. I flicked my wrist blade out, ready to strike. It didn't move.

"W-what?" I replied, suddenly realizing it wasn't trying to kill me. "I... don't understand."

It made a symbol like food, pretending to eat a sandwich. Was it asking me to eat? "G... Hungrup?" It started to move away.

I put my hat back on and followed it. "Uh, sure..."

It led me to a bonfire where the former prisoners ate uneasily with their former enemies at a long slab of rock that served as a table. They were serving cooked meat of some kind. I could only assume the Demons were cooking their own kind. The Demon who'd fetched me sat me at the head of the table, and the others all bowed their heads. A hooded stranger sat next to me. "Call me crazy, but I think you're the new chief."

I huffed tiredly. "I think so."

"You should be more excited. You have a whole army in the palm of your hand!"

"I mean... I suppose it's possible, but I can't stay here. I need to transfer power."

"It's your tribe. What you say goes."

"If they can understand what... Oh! I can teach these Demons English!"

The stranger laughed. "Is it that easy?"

I shrugged. "I mean, it shouldn't be terrible right? Just a little something before I leave this place. I don't think I could even leave without settling this." A piece of meat longer than my forearm was placed in front of me. It was the biggest at the table. Benefits of being the chief. I started eating slowly, enjoying the food with my new tribe.

The next day, I put the prisoners to work teaching the Demons English. It was like a community center. I loved it. Over the next week the Demons spoke like us more and more. It was shockingly easy, since the Demons were smart when it came to language. In that time, they got the basics down. Eventually, I chose the creature that spoke the best English and told him to follow me.

"Hmm... Your language is strange, Chief," he said. His voice was rough.

"I know. What's your name?"

"Hmm... I was called Selfton."

"Selfton. Cool. Tell me about being chief."

"We as a people follow one person. What he says, goes. We follow him, obey his commands."

"Do you mesh well with other tribes?"

Selfton scoffed. "No. They betray who we are. They fought against us. The traitors are scum. They do nothing. Where are they now?"

"Not here, that's for sure. Things won't change over in Nevada. I won't be fighting any more chiefs."

The Demon nodded. "What's the plan, Chief?"

"I'm gonna make you chief after the English lessons are over, ok?"

He shook his head, shocked. "N-no, I couldn't possibly..."

"Nonsense. You were here longer than me. Just two things: no more sacrifices and no more Angel Waste. Got it?"

"Easier said than done, chief. We've been doing both for so long. But we'll try."

I patted his shoulder. "And that's the first step to change."

Once the week was up, I taught the Demons properly. They could finally communicate with us now. Not exactly fluently, but simple sentences assisted by hand gestures. At the same time, Selfton taught me Demon. Or the basic form of it. I also learned the different markings the Demons drew.

I gave the leadership role to Selfton. The Demons bowed to him as I headed over to the old path out of the canyon. I picked up a wrapped-up Sera and turned to inform the others. I expected the former prisoners to follow me, but they stayed. I approached Okuda. "You're not leaving?"

"No," he answered. "I like it here. These Demons are ok. I'm pretty happy."

I smiled. "Wow. I can't believe it. Good luck, friend." I shook his hand and started walking away. I turned for the last time, looking at the crowd of Demons and humans, chatting and eating in harmony over the campfire. I gave them one last wave and made my way out of the canyon, Sera's body over my shoulder.

*Looks like I've solved racism.*

# CHAPTER FIFTY-THREE

## HERE'S TO YOU…

I started my hike back to the camp with my old lover in my arms. I was happy about the new tribe. Once I headed back to Nevada things would be back to the usual kill-or-be-killed mentality,  but at least I'd be able to understand the Demons before they blew my head off. Arizona would definitely be better now with the new crew. The massive sacrifices would stop, at least. I kept my pace up, walking through the sand-covered landscape.

I didn't take the time to soak in the view on the trail. I was somewhat refreshed, but really tired overall. My clothes were stained with green blood from the mini war. I was still beaten. The wounds had scabbed over, but they had yet to fully heal. After walking for a few hours, I squatted and rested next to an old restroom with Sera. I took my hat off and soaked in what had happened. I looked over, gritting my teeth. It sucked. It hurt. I had to bring her back to camp.

I stood and kept walking as the night started. The skies were cold and clear. The stars were nicer than usual. I felt like if I collapsed right now, I wouldn't complain. But Sera wouldn't like it if I dropped her right now.

I hiked for a few more hours, and reached our camp  in the middle of the night. Fisher was keeping watch. He flicked his cigarette away and sprinted toward me. "Dopeman! What happened? It's been a week! Where's… Sera…" He looked down at the wrapped body in my hands.

"No…" He shook his head. I set her down. "No! NO!" he cried hysterically, in a rush of emotion and heartbreak. Kyle and the soldiers ran out, hearing the commotion. They stopped as they saw her body. I placed my arm around Fisher, comforting him.

We stayed like this for an hour. After he fell asleep, I picked him up and put him down in his tent, then went to sleep in my own.

The next day, I was sitting with Kyle. I explained everything that happened in the canyon. Kyle popped a cigarette in his mouth. "Huh. What a story." He blew out the smoke, looking at the sky. He held the lit ciggy in his robot hand. "you're telling me that you can do all that? Why the hell do you deliver mail all day?" His voice held an unusual tone.

I shrugged. "I told you I dislike war. And since when did you smoke? I thought you tried to keep yourself clean."

"You know, I remember when I was training. I was keeping my body up fresh and in shape for people I didn't even see. I never saw the general again, after he recruited me. Then I lost my arm. All I got was a new arm and no breaks. Then I got pushed to Arizona. I lose almost all of my soldiers, I fight Demons and NRF for months and just feel like crap. While I was waiting for you, I was offered a cigarette by one of my men." He smiled. "Who cares? What're they going to do, fire me? I'm going home in two weeks anyways." He offered me the box.

I shrugged and grabbed his box and lighter. "I hate war."

"Me too, Dopeman. Me too."

I laughed. "So, what are ya gonna do once you head back?"

"See my kid. They can discharge me for all I care."

"Man, it's sad to see the young military man turn into a hardened rebel."

He scoffed as he took a drag. "Don't get me wrong, I'm loyal to the army. I will always be a Miller Corps man. I still believe in their vision of a return to democracy. I'm just going to do it..."

"Your way?" I put up a fist.

"My way." He fist-bumped me.

Later, I walked over to Fisher's tent. He hadn't been outside all day. I walked in to see the man in bed, quietly crying. I sat on the bed, placing a hand on his arm. "It's my fault. If I could've—"

"No. Don't say that." He moved to sit next to me, wiping his eyes. "Please don't say that. You did all you could. You're so strong and loyal and capable." He welled up, resting his head on my shoulders. "I always wanted to be like you ever since I saw you fight. You bring your all. Don't say anything like that again."

"Fisher, what are you trying to say?"

He looked at me. "I like you, Dopeman. Ever since I saw how much of a man I wish I could be."

"Fisher... You're funny, a good shooter, a fun guy. You don't have to be me..."

He smiled. "I don't know if you like people like me, ya know?"

I shrugged. "I never tried it. I mean… I'm pretty willing. I didn't hate the kiss…"

He held my chin. "Wanna do it again?"

I shrugged and moved in for a kiss. We locked lips for a passionate smooch for a few minutes. We pulled away, smiling. "Not bad," I said.

Fisher smiled and playfully smacked my face. "Glad it wasn't terrible."

Later that night, the soldiers gathered and we burned Sera's body. I watched the fire, crying. I stood and walked to the front of the congregation, then spoke. "Sera was a caregiver. She always wanted to take care of me, of all of us. She was the mother of Miller Corps. She was a fighter till the end. She would be proud of us. All of us. Sera was… my anchor. She was the reason I didn't break down in these wars. She was the reason I was recovering as quickly as I could. I loved her…" I paused. Then I wiped my face. "We will all drink in her name. Here's to Sera, mother of the Miller Corps!"

They all chanted.

*Here's to you, Sera.*

# CHAPTER FIFTY-FOUR

## BREAK TAKERS

Peace.

Or something close to it.

For now. I felt like I could breathe. I started smoking with Fisher and Kyle. We drank and talked long into the night.

We were sitting around a campfire one night, laughing at the story of my tournament exploits.

"Wait," Kyle put his hands up, chuckling like a fool. "You're telling me you lost, after all that?"

I shrugged as I took a puff of the cancer stick. "That woman was overpowered. She could kill anybody in there. If there hadn't been a rule against it, I would be dead. Most likely."

Sam chimed in. "Tell the last part, bro. That was the best part."

"So, here we are, kicking each other's asses, right? I was on the floor, then I got this sudden burst of life. We fought and struggled some more. I had her in this chokehold..."

"Kinky," Fisher joked. The group had a good chuckle.

"Shut up! As I was saying, I was choking her out, but I was so low on strength and blood, I passed out. I was gone. She won."

Kyle took my cig and popped it into his mouth. "Shame, shame. You know, that's a good idea. We should do that, but not as bloody."

I nodded and laughed. "There has to be a prize. Like a nice clock."

"Something better than a clock." Fisher held up a nice unopened pack of cigars. We looked at it with shock. "Pre. War. Cigars." Since every single man and woman in the camp was a chronic smoker now, they would get in on this in a heartbeat.

I took the pack in my hands. "Perfect."

Kyleagreed. "I'll get some rounds ready tomorrow."

We eventually headed back to our tents. I was drinking a glass of water when Mox came up to me. "Hey, Dopeman."

"Yo. Need something?"

"Yeah. I overheard your conversation."

"You want the cigars, don't you?"

"Of course! I haven't had one in years. That wonderful tobacco... Geez..."

I chuckled. "Oh relax, boss. What did you need?"

Mox adjusted her feet as we reached my tent. "Were you planning on joining the tournament?"

I shook my head. "I had my fair share of tournaments already. I'm not stepping foot in another ring."

"That sounds good. Then you wouldn't mind helping me with my fighting skills, yeah?"

"Hm? I thought the NRF taught you close-quarters combat pretty well."

Mox made a face. "Eh, well I can assume we're fighting for a crowd, yeah?"

I nodded. I assumed the tournament would have a few eyes on it.

"That's the problem. I'm not a huge fan of crowds and performances. You've won. I want to know how you did that."

It wasn't late. I could throw her a few pointers before I went to bed. "Sure. Let's go on open land." I finished my drink and walked with her to an open piece of desert.

"Now," I started as I removed my hat and sand cape. "I want you to picture something for me. Close your eyes."

She shut her eyes slowly.

"I want you to picture us in that circle. I'm in front of you, just like now. I looked focused, in the zone. What do you hear right now?"

"Nothing..."

"Wrong. You hear the chanting of the crowd. The men and women surround you. They're drunk, loud. It's been hours. They've been cooking in the hot sun watching fights and bloodshed. They've seen both our defeats and victories. These animals are half and half on who's gonna win. Sure, half cheer and help you on, but the other half boo you, want you dead. They want you on the ground, knocked out. You know what you should do?"

She shook her head. She looked panicked.

"Ignore it all. Even the positive ones. I want you to think back to this moment. This moment of silence. This moment of loneliness. This technique makes you block out everyone. The only thing you will see is your opponent and yourself. I call this... The Age of Loneliness. Now open your eyes."

Her eyelids snapped up. "The Age of Loneliness?"

"It's saying it's just you and your opponent. I only hear the crowd before the fight, and during, they might as well be dead."

Mox smiled, thinking about the concept. "I like it... I think I can do this."

"The only real way you can get the technique is to try it out on the battlefield."

"Thanks, Dopeman. Now, did you wanna spar?"

I shrugged and smiled. "Why not? Let's get a couple of hits in."

She charged me instantly. She used her legs almost exclusively. I blocked all I could, even dodging a few kicks. Then she caught me in the jaw. I turned and swept her legs out from under her, getting on top of her and aiming a few soft hits at her face. We both laughed as I helped her up. "Nice kicking, Mox."

We headed back to the campsite. "How did you get so good at fighting, Dopeman?"

"I'm not a good fighter. I just learned to fight my way."

"What is your way?"

"Cheating." I laughed. "But that's my last piece of advice. Before you do anything, you make sure to do it your way."

"I'll keep that in mind." She kissed my cheek. "Night, Dopeman."

I waved and headed back into my tent to sleep.

The next day Kyle called out to the group. "Listen up. After everything that's happened, I know you folks need a break and a chance to relax, so I got a little competition. Combat!" He pulled out leather pads. The soldiers smiled and nudged each other. "The prize is a nice box of cigars. Not just any, pre-war!" The crowd oohed and ahhed. "We need sixteen people. Any takers?"

The spots  filled pretty quickly,Mox included. I gathered with the spectators, watching the crowd as we drank booze. I was becoming a stronger drinker. I saw my girl beat all the competition with her mighty legs. She kicked her way to the finals.I yelled out what I said last night in my state of drunkenness. "THE AGE! THE AGE!!"

She closed her eyes and huffed. Once she opened them, she was in the zone. She won the tournament.

Now I needed to snag a cigar.

# CHAPTER FIFTY-FIVE

## ON THE ROAD HOME

It was another crazy night, that's for sure. It was a night of fun, jokes, and cigar smoke. After Mox kicked her opponent out, we charged up to hug her. We chanted her name and someone started banging the drums. Mox ran to break out the pack of cigars and threw some into the crowd. I caught one, naturally. I pulled out my lighter to smoke it. It wasn't that bad, actually.

We continued the party all night. I danced, drank, and fought with some of the soldiers. After a long night of booze and relentless singing, I passed out.

I woke up covered in booze. I smelled. I felt pretty bad, but that was ok. I'd had the time of my life. I watched a fight, I had a party. What more could I ask for, really? I looked around to see the crowd still knocked out or wandering. I stood up and walked around the camp, looking for my friends. I saw Kyle, sitting at a table with sunken eyes and a mug in his hand. He had his head down. "D-Dopeman..."

I sat next to him. "Kyle. Here I thought you had a stronger will than me."

"I can stand intense torture for more than three months, but I can't stand a night of drinking."

"Wait, you survived torture?"

He burped and downed the water. "Long story."

I laughed as he groaned. Then I walked away, looking for more of my friends. It wasn't too long before I saw Fisher asleep on the ground. A cigar was still in his mouth. I kicked him. He groaned. "W-What…?"

I squatted. "Rise and shine. You're asleep on the ground. You probably shouldn't do that."

"It's comfortable. Come on, man. Let me sleep…"

"Come on, handsome." I helped the Fisherman up and over to his tent. He kissed me as I sat him on the bed. "You're gonna be lazy all day?" I joked.

"Cut me a break. Or I'll have to do more than kissing this time." He winked.

I laughed and headed out of the tent, looking for my champion. I popped a cig in my mouth as I did my grand walk around the camp. Eventually, I found her, looking at the afternoon sun. She was laying on top of a table, enjoying the last cigar. "Hey, champ." I lay down next to her. She looked proud.

"Hey, coach." She tapped my shoulder and laughed.

"Coach? Ha! Good one. But you did well. I'm proud."

"Thanks. I appreciate the lesson you taught me."

"It's just something simple, ya know? A block-out technique."

"When did you learn that?"

"The Age of Loneliness? It's something I learned from my fights in the old world."

"What, you were a prizefighter?"

"Nah. Before I dropped out of school I fought a lot. I was a small kid so I was a target."

She sat up. "Tell me more."

"So, there was this one time, I was going to use the bathroom. It was a regular day. Then some punk came in the door with a crowd. He'd been targeting me for a while. I was always the one fighting back against him. Everyone had their cameras out, ready to record. I was shoved into this position for the first time. I had all those phone lights on me, all those kids screaming. It was sensory overload. To make it worse, the big man was itching to embarrass me. He was punching me all over the bathroom. I couldn't focus. I wanted the noise to stop, I wanted to be..."

"Alone."

I nodded. "At once, everything was just gone. It was me and him. With a bloody nose and new focus, I punched the fool right in the gut. He coughed violently. I hit him with a right hook. I kept on with that hook till he bled. I finished him off by punching him into the mirror. He was out. I was so upset I kicked him in the head."

"Wow. What a story. You must have a crazy back story."

I chuckled. "Well, That's me. I wonder, what made you so scared of crowds?"

Mox hugged her arm. "Eh, I was in a play once. I was playing the leading lady. I was on the stage saying my final monologue when I blew chunks. All over the stage. I was so terrified of all the eyes on me ya know?"

"Oh yeah, I get it. I'm glad I taught you right. Stay safe, okay?" I said, hugging her.

"You too, Dopeman."

It was only a few days later when the helicopters finally came.

We all cheered as they landed. Kyle, Fisher and I packed all of our gear and whatever we could carry and got on our helicopter. As we flew up in the air, I looked over the canyon for the last time. I never thought I would, but I smiled. I hoped the tribe would prosper and spread peace throughout the rest of Arizona. We flew over Lake Retals. I hoped the Shaman could meet the new tribe. I also hoped he'd stop making people smoke. That was dangerous.

We flew over Roach National Park. It was a crappy place overall, especially with those sacrifices. And finally, we reached the factory. Where this madness started. It was a ghost town. I looked over to my crew. Kyle and Fisher gave me weak smiles. They were tired, like me. I laughed. "I hate Arizona."

"That canyon was overrated," Fisher commented.

Kyle grinned. "I'll take Nevada any day of the week."

I gave a thumbs up. "Amen to that."

We landed a few hours later in Badlands. I stepped out to look at the old village. A few months ago, I was the Foolish Courier. I delivered packages from Compton. As I walked out of the airfield, I was greeted by an old man. He was a decorated military man. Had tons of metals. He shook my hand. "Dopeman, in the flesh. It's a pleasure to meet you."

I shake his hand and nod. "Thank you. You must be—"

"General Miller."

My eyes widened.

*Oh my.*

# CHAPTER FIFTY-SIX
## NEVADA FUTURE

We walked to General Miller's office.

The room was as nice as it could be for a post-war room. It had one desk and two chairs on both sides. It had a few shelves, stocked with binders and maps and rounds of ammo. As for decorations, they were littered all over the room. They were medals that had been  preserved throughout the years. I was surprised that the medals had been saved, let alone preserved in such good condition. I sat in the chair opposite the desk. I looked out of place. My clothes were still stained from all the fights I'd had. Miller noticed my discomfort. "Problem?"

I shook my head. "It's just been a while since I've been anywhere decent looking."

He laughed. "I see. So, Dopeman. I've been gathering information on you, naturally, while you made waves in the south. You were the Foolish Courier. A man with a bounty on his head delivering packages across the wasteland. You currently have about five to six hundred thousand gold on your head. That's partly the reason you joined up with the Miller Corps, according to Major Tann's report. That same day you had two more volunteers join you. Together, you call yourselves Team Foolish."

"General, I understand you read up on me, but what's the point? Not like I'm in your ranks."

Miller leaned back in his chair. "There is a point to everything, Dopeman. I know you. But do you know what we fight for?"

"Yeah, you fight to bring democracy to the west."

Miller looked satisfied. "Now, the war is far from over. Whatever you've done in Arizona has put them on the ropes. I want you in my army as a major. You'd be an invaluable piece."

I smiled. This was a big offer. I could be free from any future bounty, I could get a respectable job and spread the legend of Dopeman.

I gave the only answer I could. "No."

Miller looked slightly surprised. "No?"

"Nope. You know, when I was walking the desert, I had no purpose. The girl I loved was dead. I had this guilt that wouldn't go away. I'd been a drug dealer in the past. I sold crack and I ruined my community. I had gained the riches I dreamed of at the expense of my own people, chief. I was the dopeman. But here I am after all this, kind of in the same spot. The girl I love is dead. But...I feel no guilt. I think I've forgiven myself. I've gone through hell and back to help you out, so I think I just want to be Dopeman, the courier." I stood and turned to leave.

"Wait," he said before I stepped out. "You've done so much for this army in such a short time. The least I can do is clear the bounty. Now, whenever you change your mind, there's always a space open."

"Don't hold your breath."

I headed out of the tent, looking into the Nevada sunset. It's nice to see you again, I thought. I missed the heat.

I saw Kyle sitting at a table, signing a few papers. Once he was done, he walked with me. "I'm on leave. I can finally take a vacation."

"Sounds good. Speaking of, I'm gonna tag along with you for a bit."

"Oh? Why?"

"I assume the first thing you're gonna do is head over to your wife."

He nodded. "Pretty much. She hired you to take that letter to me, right?"

"Mhm. I just wanna complete one more mission before I take my vacation."

He laughed. We walked over to his house as I told him about my conversation with Miller. He seemed surprised by the offer, but not at all by my reply. He knew me.

He walked up to the door of his house and knocked. The house was small and well-built, with tan paint cracking due to the weather. The door was answered by a young woman. She was pretty obviously pregnant. She looked at her husband, eyes welling with tears, and she smiled. She kissed Kyle, not caring about how dirty he was. That's real love. Then she looked down to see his metal arm. "Baby... your..."

"I know," he said, looking disappointed. "I'm so sorry. I was trying my best."

"As long as you're alive." She looked over at me. "Oh! Foolish Courier! Or is it Dopeman?"

I shrugged. "It's Dopeman. No problem. I can see why you married the stubborn man."

She smiled and pulled the gold she owed me out of her pocket. "Here."

I took it happily. "Thank you."

Kyle tapped my back. "Did you plan on staying in town?"

"Um, yeah. I like it here."

"You're gonna need more gold, then." He went into the house and came out with  more gold. "It might buy you a few nights at a hotel."

I felt so grateful. "Thanks. I mean really, thanks."

"You've done so much for me, Dopeman. I'll see you around. Maybe we can get a drink some time."

Once the happy couple headed in, I walked away. Mission complete.

I walked into a water bar to sit and reflect. I needed to find Harper. She had Serena as well. As I drank my water, my dear old friend tapped my shoulder. "Dopeman!"

"Harper!" I hugged her. She smelled nice. She had a white and blue style going on, with her white shirt and blue dress pants.

"I got a little home I'm squatting in with your horse."

"Serena? I missed her. She's a good horse, ain't she?"

"You sound like you're in love, weirdo."

I looked at the woman and grinned. "Maybe I am."

"Shut up," she said, giggling.

# CHAPTER FIFTY-SEVEN

## DOPEMAN

We walked out of the bar as the stars came out. Harper led me to a decent little shack. I spotted Serena. She neighed happily and cantered to me, almost running me over.

"Serena!" I hugged her head and kissed her forehead. "I missed you so much!"

Serena neighed sincerely. She was comfortable with me. I felt the same. Harper took a little note in her book and walked into the house. I did the same, with Serena hanging outside looking in a large window. I sat down next to the window. Harper sat on a chair and began writing a few things. "You look disgusting. You gotta take a bath soon."

"It's been a long day. That I can say. Give me a few."

She nodded and continued working. I walked outside to the washing pool. I got in the bath and relaxed. It was cold that night, but I didn't care. It felt amazing. I felt all the stress fade away. I had time to reflect. For now, all I could do was  enjoy my vacation. I thought for now, I might work on the west coast. I was  way too tired to be going across the country.

After finishing in the bath, I washed my clothes and hung them on the wire. I put on my underwear and walked in, sitting down. "So, what's new, Harper?"

"Ah, the usual. I was doing everything to figure out what you did in Arizona for your operation. I released a few issues of Desertland news. Those caught fire, let me tell you. Everyone wanted to see the cool guy with the cape and the special shotgun fight in a war. You got a following, that's for sure."

"Wow. I never thought that I'd lose the old name."

"You did. Everyone in town knows about Dopeman. They love the stories too. I think you can capitalize."

"How so?" I asked.

"I want you to write a book."

"You want me to write? Like a whole novel?"

Harper tapped my hand. "What? Don't you like reading, Dopeman?"

"I love reading. I read about rifles, history, and even fiction. Serena! What was that one book called?"

Serena neighed informatively.

"That! Yeah, that."

Harper looked at me, confused. "You can understand her?"

"Yes."

She stared at me. "You really need to write this book."

"Look, look. I need to think about how to start. It's a lot of stories to tell."

"Sleep on it, ok? You'll be fine. The thing about writing is that you can't force it out. You can't figure it out like that. It comes naturally. Once those first few words pop into your head, it'll be as natural as breathing."

"Hmm…" I mumbled, and moved to rest on the old couch. I needed to sleep on it. I said goodnight to my friend and slept pretty well for the first time in months.

The next day, I opened my eyes and sighed happily. I thought I would never feel this good, ever again. I got up and walked around the house. Harper was still asleep, so I ] went outside to put on my sort-of clean gear. I stretched before walking out into the hot Nevada day.

I headed over to a more populated water bar. A lot of people greeted me, told me how cool I looked, and I did my best to smile and wave, making sure all of the people felt the love. I even got free water. I was pretty happy. It was then that Fisher showed up. The people had heard of him too, and gave a warm greeting.

"Sup, Sam," I said as he sat with me.

"I'm right as rain. How's it going? Enjoying the vacation?"

"Oh yeah. I had some sleep, talked with my friend. She's a journalist and wants me to write a novel."

"A novel? About your life or something?"

"Yeah. I never wrote like this before. Or at all, even. I wrote essays and whatever for school. Just never a novel. I don't even know how to start it."

"Why don't you start at the beginning?"

"What even is the beginning? Pre-war? Intro wars?"

"No, no. Your beginning. Your start. How did this whole journey start?"

I thought about it for a moment. "I guess you could say it started in Compton."

"How so?" Fisher asked.

"I mean, I was there for a job. I took the train from here to Compton in order to complete a job. After blowing up a saloon I took the train back. It was there I met Harper."

He chuckled. "Sounds like a Dopeman story. If that's the start of this madness, then you write your truth."

I finished my water and moved to leave. "Thanks, Fisher. Plan on staying in town?"

"Of course. Might as well. I don't know if I should continue the fight with Miller Corps. I think I might relax with you folk. Maybe take you out sometime?"

I laughed out loud. "Maybe. I'll see ya around."

I made my way over to the house again to see Harper typing, as usual. "Welcome back, hero. Thought of something?"

I sat on the couch. "I think. I think I need a title, most importantly."

"Okay, like what?"

I looked at my hands, looked at the floor. I looked at everything, everyone. Who am I?

Who am I?

That's easy.

"DOPEMAN," I said.

"Really? I like it. It's simple. I'll give you a notebook." Harper walked into her room, then came out and handed me a notebook and a pen. I grabbed the pen and clicked it a few times. My handwriting was awful, but here we were.

If I was starting in Compton, where should I start?

On the train? The hike to town? No, the barn!

I knew exactly how to start.

"The day was hot. The sun beamed down on me, it felt like Satan himself was in bed with me..."

# EPILOGUE
## A NOTE FROM YOUR PAL, DOPEMAN

Hey! It's Dopeman!

Since it's been a few months since I last wrote, I'd better inform you all of what's new.

Baby Grant was born. He's so cute! I'm a proud uncle. Kyle took an extended leave to be in his son's life. He's never been happier.

Sam wanted to stay with me, so it was easy to help him build a nice home next to us. Despite everything, he still wants to date me. I gave him a chance, we're going steady.

Speaking of homes, I live with Harper and Serena in a place way nicer than Harper's shack. Sam helped us build it. I love them both to death; just waking up is a joy now.

I also wanna thank all of the people who helped me individually.

**To the entire Tann family:** Thank you for making me better with kids, making me a better fighter, a better leader, and happier.

**To Sam aka Fisher:** You made me laugh countless times through it all. From getting burned by the waste through the worst parts of Arizona. You're also not a bad kisser.

**To Harper:** Without you, I wouldn't even have had the idea to write this entire thing. You were there. From draft to completion. You're smarter than I could ever be. So, thanks for everything.

**To Dani:** You made me realize my humanity. I wasn't just some machine. I wasn't the Dopeman. I was more than that. I was my own person. I still love you.

**To Sera:** You reminded me I had people who actually cared for me. For a long time, I thought I was alone. I had nobody. You changed that. You also helped me move on from my bad past. I was better than that. I'm better now. My heart will always be with you.

**To Carter, Genny, and Kaos, and the prisoners:** You all helped me get tougher. Become a man in tip-top shape. Genny, Kaos. If you two are reading this, come on by. I'd love to catch up.

I figured I can use these last few lines in the notebook to write a little monologue. Is my story complete? Nah. Not by a long shot. I have so many stories to tell everyone. If there are any little kids reading this story and feeling inspired by me pushing through my limits and breaking my body to get the job done, I have one thing to say. Don't be like me. Be better than me. I made bad choices, I'll admit. Those mistakes cost people's limbs and lives. You learn from my mistakes.

You're never alone.

Your pal,

*Dopeman*


THE END

# ABOUT THE AUTHOR

Maurice Campbell was born in Milwaukee, Wisconsin on January 26th, 2002. As a kid, he was introverted with an active imagination. He often lived in his own head a lot. This manifested into a writing hobby when he was a sophomore in high school.

A hobby turned into a passion as he found himself writing more as the 2020s hit. In 2020, he made LoveHER and Descent. In 2021, for a writing contest, he made DOPEMAN.

Maurice hopes to share his stories to the world, and inspire that kid stuck in his own head to express himself, and share their stories too.

Thank you for reading a MoonQuill original novel. To experience more exciting stories, visit us at moonquill.com

To know when we release new books, join our mailing list from our site and receive three books for free!
We will never spam you!

To talk with other members of the MoonQuill community, check out our community Discord.

Finally, we would really appreciate it if you could take a moment to review the book. Every review greatly helps the author and supports their ability to continue writing fantastic books for us to enjoy.